CW01465345

THE NAME OF THE GAME

QUEENS OF THE STEAL
VOLUME ONE, PART ONE

IJ BENNEYWORTH

Also by IJ Benneyworth

The Amanda Northstar Mysteries

Dark River

Heads Will Roll

With thanks to my scribe tribe for their feedback and advice and to Marta for her ever vigilant eye for detail!

FOLLOW IJ BENNEYWORTH ON THE WEB AND SOCIAL MEDIA:

Web: www.scribecorps.com

Facebook: IJ Benneyworth Books

Twitter: @scribecorps

FIND AND FOLLOW DOUG HILLS AT:

Web: dnhills.com

Twitter: @DNHills

Author's Note

Firstly dear reader, a heartfelt thanks from me for purchasing this work. While I confess I'd love to make a full-time career out of writing, I do this mainly for pleasure. Since I was a young boy, I've derived joy from exploring new worlds and characters on the big and small screens, on the written page, and crafting my own. I would regularly sit with my grandfather in his parlor. He would prompt me to continue a verbal story he had started, adjusting it to reflect my additions and then passing it back to progress. Though a simple and fun exercise for a six-year-old, it was an early introduction to forming characters, worlds, and storylines. It helped me think about basic narrative structure and character motivations, even if it only involved my grandfather's alter ego Alfie and his companion Freddy figuring out how to traverse a jungle or escape from crocodiles.

I remember overhearing my grandfather remarking to my grandmother in their kitchen that I would become a writer one day. So it was a proud and joyous moment when I eventually published my first novel, a murder mystery called *Dark River*, in 2016. Its protagonist was Amanda Northstar, sheriff of a fictional town and county in the Hudson Valley. A year later, its sequel, *Heads Will Roll*, was released. As much as I love *Dark River* for being my first literary child, I feel now as I did at the time that *Heads Will Roll* is the superior thriller. I enjoyed writing its faster pace, exciting set-pieces, and race-against-time situations. I will return to Amanda's world one day. However, I wanted to scratch the thriller itch, and so this is why you are currently holding *Queens of the Steal*.

I like heist movies, especially clever ones where you wonder how they got away with it. Queens represents an experiment for me. Balancing more characters than ever without sacrificing their depth, playing around with time in the narrative, writing thrilling action scenes and, the big one, serializing it into multiple parts. Think of it as a literary television show. What you're about to read is the pilot. There will be seven more parts in Volume One, each self-contained but forming a more expansive story arc. Hopefully, Volumes Two and Three will complete the masterplan. My point is that you have kindly bought Part One, and so be rest assured that, though some may take longer than others, forthcoming parts will be written and published. There will be an ending to the story you are about to begin. I hope it, and the Archer sisters, captivate you enough to return to find out how they pull off that one last job.

IJ Benneyworth,
September 2020

"The number one rule of thieves
is that nothing is too small to steal."

- Jimmy Breslin

"Thieves respect property. They merely wish
the property to become their property that
they may more perfectly respect it."

- Gilbert K. Chesterton

PROLOGUE

The warehouse was unusually humid for late October, but she didn't mind. Angelina Archer - she insisted on Angie - was a summer girl. She always had been and always would be. The summer months meant longer days and extra hours to run, to explore, to let her thoughts wander as she watched the setting sun glimmer on the surface of the East River before sprinting home to keep her promise of never staying out after dark.

Angie had lost count of the number of times she had sat under the shadow of the east side of the Brooklyn Bridge and watched as other people, ordinary people, went about their lives. She enjoyed looking on at mothers walking with their children. Whereas others may have been bitter, Angie was thankful, grateful that those kids didn't know the pain that she felt. There were still times, though, when envy intruded on her thoughts. It would whisper into her ear that those other kids didn't have to worry about whether their whole family would return home after going to work.

The four monsters make ready, checking their weapons; Colt AR-15 semi-automatic assault rifles, a military and law enforcement workhorse. Clicks and clacks fill the van's rear as thirty-round magazines are drawn from ammunition pouches on belts, the 5.56mm rounds inside checked, the magazines slotted into rifles, the cocking levers pulled back, the application of safety catches confirmed. The masks they wear are perfect seasonal disguises, the same mass-manufactured ghouls found in stores across New York City with Halloween imminent, impossible to trace.

Dracula, the leader, looks upon his three teammates in the gloom of the rear compartment. It stinks of bleach, a precaution to wash away lingering DNA, not that there should be any. He has taught his team well, attention to detail in everything, a backup plan at all times. The van is the primary getaway vehicle, stolen from a telecoms company and disposable, to be torched if necessary or crushed if time allows. A sedan from the late-Nineties is parked in a back alley a block away as a secondary option. It's old but reliable, non-flashy, easy to blend in with.

'Same play as usual, just remember our moves,' says Dracula in a matter-of-fact way, trying to calm the group's nerves as their adrenaline begins to flow.

He knows this because he also feels it. He has for every mission on behalf of Uncle Sam or score in aid of himself. He realizes he could be only minutes away from death in the worst case, but the rush when everything comes off? It's one of the only things that make him feel alive these days, temporarily suppressing the pain and pressure that grind him down from dawn to dusk. He hates it and loves it at the same time. Patriot and criminal, a father who loves his children but puts them in danger by what he does. He knows he is a contradiction but has learned to accept it, or perhaps he just ignores it.

It wasn't always that way. At first, he embraced the life to put food on the table, or so he told himself. Pride was a factor, of not wanting to work some menial job when the skills he had developed could make him so much more than a nine-to-five ever would. But then came cancer, his wife ravaged by it, their savings gone in *months. It stopped being about his pride and became all about her survival, paying medical bills that endlessly assaulted their finances like waves crashing against cliffs. All the money in the world can't sustain a body that doesn't want to be saved.*

Now she's gone, but her legacy, his children, live on and he wants the best future for them that money can buy. That desire makes him a good father, but the way he's achieving it makes him a bad one. But, like the pain he wakes up with every morning in a half-empty bed, he'll momentarily forget that inner conflict as the thrill of the job takes him and the adrenaline washes over.

He raises a thumbs up. Crouching opposite him, Frankenstein's Monster, the Wolfman, and the Wicked Witch of the West return the gesture. He nods.

'Let's go.'

Work. That was one word for it. What her family did every few months paid the bills and contributed to Angie's college fund. She had initially felt guilty about being one of the main drivers for the Archer clan doing what they did. That was until she realized that if it hadn't been her future they claimed to be supporting, it would have been some other justification. They were in too deep to stop. She may have been thirteen, but Angie wasn't stupid. She had gone along with the fiction but was always aware of it. If she would eventually educate herself into a safer and more prosperous life as her family said they wanted for her, then fine. Safer perhaps, but certainly more boring. All Angie could do was sit and wait in the same empty warehouse each time they went to 'work'.

The bank's main door bursts open and the monsters sweep in, all speed, surprise, and aggression. It's quieter than usual, just as planned. The morning rush has barely begun, most people still needing that strong second coffee. At first, only for a moment, the dozen or so customers and staff think some kind of seasonal practical joke is underway. Four people dressed in loose-fitting, identical black jumpsuits and duffle jackets wearing monster masks that cover their whole heads? Surely something to do with Halloween, only days away. But why wear so much to conceal themselves in this humidity? Why are they carrying those large backpacks? What are they pulling out from under their-

Dracula delivers a short, sharp gut-punch with his rifle butt to the ample stomach of one of the security guards, who crumples to the ground. He raises his weapon and aims it at the collection of bank tellers behind the counter. The other members of the monster squad fan out, their rifles also raised and ready.

'Down on the fuckin' ground, now!' roars Dracula as many of the new captives scream and whimper.

He jumps over the counter, his attention focused on one goal. The others know theirs intimately. The Wicked Witch heads straight for the rear office area to take out the hard drives recording all the security camera footage. Wolfman has already tied a zip cord around the main door's handles to prevent anyone from entering, and in seconds will locate the manager to open the vault just as the time lock is released. Finally, Frankenstein is on crowd control, herding the customers on the main floor into a central grouping, collecting their cellphones into a bag lined with magnetic tape, before zip-locking their wrists behind their backs as they lay flat on their stomachs.

However, Dracula needs to find the second security guard, so he can take over vault duties and free up Wolfman to assist with crowd control. The guard should have been on the main floor with his partner, but he's not. Dracula quickly scans the area behind the counter, sees only the suits, skirts, and blouses of the staff, as well as the manager being dragged up by Wolfman and led to the vault. There's no blue shirt, though.

Dracula turns around to check the rear office area when he comes face-to-face with the second guard carrying a coffee cup, his eyebrows raised in surprise. This isn't the second guard they expected, not the one seen every day during scouting. That guy was clearly an ex-cop on a pension, no doubt fitter and leaner than his partner, but just as unlikely to take a bullet to protect the bank's federally insured money. This guy, though, the one Dracula's rifle muzzle is only inches away from, is young and strong.

It takes only a moment for Dracula to judge that the guard is ex-military. He just has that aura about him, the way he carries himself, the neatness of his appearance, the muscularity crafted during endless workout sessions. Who knows, or indeed cares, why the guy isn't still in the services? He's standing in this bank in the *here and now, a small but unexpected element introduced into a well-crafted plan. As Dracula well knows from past missions, it's not the size of the element that can undermine a plan, it's that unexpectedness.*

At least Angie was not alone as she waited. Amidst the stacks of dusty crates that had remained unopened for years, a basic office had been constructed out of wooden beams and plywood near the main entrance. Inside the rectangular room were shelves, a desk, filing cabinets, a coffee table, and two leather armchairs. Like the supposed import-export business the warehouse hosted, the desk and filing cabinets were strictly for show. Upon the shelves, in-between various sports trophies and military memorabilia, rested photos of two young men in green combat fatigues, sometimes part of a group, often just the two of them together, whether the background was a jungle, desert or some blasted townscape. One of the men was Angie's father, Axel Archer. The other was the man sitting opposite her on the second armchair, eyeing her with playful suspicion across the coffee table as they played a game of Go Fish.

Like Axel, Jimmy Delgado was in his mid-fifties. Unlike Axel, still lean, athletic, and dashing despite the growing collection of grey hairs and emerging wrinkles, Jimmy was an oak of a man. Even though he had developed a slight paunch with age, his barrel chest and impressive biceps were a constant reminder of the robust physical force he had once been in the military. His olive skin and still-black hair and goatee betrayed his Italian pedigree. He cheerfully played to the stereotype by wearing a gold chain around his neck that half-disappeared into a thick batch of salt-and-pepper chest hair visible through his open-necked bowling shirt.

Jimmy was a second father to Angie, and the brother Axel never had. His days of joining her father on excursions were long gone, the cost of years of wear and tear in whichever hellholes the United States government has seen fit to dispatch him to, as well as a need to keep his nose clean given the antagonistic history between the

New York Police Department and the Delgado family. So Jimmy waited too, probably just as anxiously as Angie. However, she suspected it was worse for him as he knew everything about what was happening and so the risks involved. In contrast, she knew nothing except that a job was on. Angie wouldn't have been at the warehouse if one hadn't been underway, all the easier to get everyone together if something went wrong rather than pull her out of school.

Nothing ever did go wrong, though. The first Angie heard of what the Archers had been up to were various reports online or on television, describing slick jobs pulled off with great speed, minimal injury, and no fatalities. It was like sitting in a hospital, waiting to hear if a family member's surgery had been a success or not. Up to now, they had all been, but even the most skilled surgeons still had marks in the loss column. It was only a matter of time.

The bank's rear door opens, and as soon as Dracula sticks his head out to check both directions of the alleyway, a hail of bullets peppers the brickwork around him. He ducks back in, raising his arms in front of him protectively.

'Fuck!' he yells, shocked.

He's never known a job to go south as quickly as this one has. Since encountering the surprise security guard, it's taken just over fifteen minutes, and the chaotic events during those minutes, for their well-ordered, clockwork routine to turn to dust. Man plans, God laughs.

Two police cruisers are parked at either end of the back alley that runs along the rear of the building, NYPD officers letting rip with their sidearms. It's still the best bet the monsters have. If they go out the front, they'll be cut to pieces in seconds. Dracula has a backup plan, though. When you need an escape route and all the ones available are gone, make your own.

He pulls out a directed blast plate from his backpack's unzipped top compartment, the one he reserves for spare ammunition and various toys, leaving the main section below free to carry money. A disc-shaped device, the purpose of the charge is to use the explosive material distributed inside it to blast a hole through walls during raids. He turns to the three other monsters waiting behind him.

'Cover me on both sides. I'll set this for five-seconds. After it goes, don't even wait, just go through and head for the car.'

The other monsters nod. Frankenstein and Wolfman crouch down to reduce themselves as targets and dash past Dracula, setting themselves up to shoot while kneeling. Their AR-15's set to burst fire, they squeeze the triggers, releasing short, disciplined volleys. The high walls of the alleyway make the reporting of the gunfire deafening. Their bullets tear into the NYPD cruisers, peppering the doors with bullet holes, penetrating the engine blocks, and shattering glass and plastic.

The police officers duck and cover, though they are not deliberately targeted. The monsters don't kill cops or any innocents for that matter. It's Dracula's main rule. Controlled violence may be needed to get the job done, but only fools, psychos, and those without a plan employ the lethal kind. It's a principle that's served them well on every job, if only to sustain their belief that they're not really bad guys in the grand scheme. But then they've never been in this tight a spot before and, after what just went down inside the bank, Wolfman wouldn't bet against this situation spiraling entirely out of control.

As they lay down covering fire, Dracula dashes across the alley, fixes the blast charge to the brick wall directly opposite the bank's rear entrance, sets the timer going, and dives back inside.

'Cover!' he yells.

Frankenstein and Wolfman, already on their feet, bound back in behind him and slam the door shut. With a deafening crack, the blast charge ignites, blowing a hole in the wall and scattering dust and debris in both directions down the alley. Within a second, the bank door opens again, and the four monsters pour out. They use the dust cloud to their advantage to conceal their escape as they duck through the new opening and dodge still-falling brick fragments. On the other side, they find themselves in a half-filled gravel parking lot. All they need to do is get through this area, work their way down a few more alleyways, and reach the backup car.

The crew runs as fast as their burning lungs allow, their weaponry and bags of money weighing heavily. Their masks limit *how much air they can eagerly suck in. They dive to the ground in unison as the glass of half a dozen cars around them explodes, and the crack of gunfire rings out once again. However, this time, the fire is not from 9mm semi-automatic pistols, but assault rifles just like theirs, capable of going fully automatic and shredding them in seconds. The NYPD's Emergency Services Unit, the ESU, otherwise known as SWAT to Joe Public, is on their heels, having decided not to simply wait at the front of the bank when all hell was breaking loose at the rear.*

Dracula rises and rests his rifle on the trunk of one of the cars, unleashing a sustained volley that rips into the vehicles near the ESU team, sending them scattering or diving behind cover. The other monsters know precisely what to do, the routine having been drilled into them repeatedly. Witch and Wolfman pick themselves up, dash as far and as fast as possible, and slide across the gravel ground to a stop. Frankenstein bear-crawls over to Dracula and crouches down next to him, occasionally popping up to release short, sharp volleys. Assuming positions behind some cars a few meters apart from each other, the first two monsters scream 'Go!' before laying down fire on the ESU team's position. Dracula and

Frankenstein cease their own firing, rise, and sprint past Witch and Wolfman, stopping a dozen yards further down and taking up their own firing positions once again.

The monsters are now as they should be, two providing covering fire while the other pair leapfrog past them and reload, repeating as needed. The ESU team does its best to return fire and inch forward. Still, the monsters are disciplined and accurate, as well-oiled as their weaponry, their volleys virtually continuous as dozens of car bodies are torn into, windows explode, gravel is kicked up from the ground and spent brass bullet casings mix in with the brown autumn leaves that blow in the gentle breeze.

'Prepare to move!' screams Wolfman, the exit of the parking lot's perimeter fence only a dozen yards away and beyond that an alleyway that will lead them to the backup car.

'Move!' comes the call and Wolfman and Witch rise up and sprint towards Frankenstein and Dracula as they lay down covering fire.

The exit to the fence is so close now, it'll only take seconds to reach, then maybe another minute or so to get to the car. What happens then, Wolfman can only guess. It can't be any worse than *the shit show this morning has turned into. Just get to the car first, then Witch can work the usual magic behind the wheel. They can get back to the warehouse, catch their breath, and discuss what the hell just happened back at the bank.*

Wolfman hears the crunch of gravel and a grunt, instantly turning to find that Witch has tripped and fallen to the ground. Wolfman skids to a halt and doubles back, extending a hand for Witch, who reaches up.

Suddenly all Wolfman can see is the sky as the bullet hits.

It was because Angie preferred to stay off her laptop during these periods of waiting, to take a break from practicing her coding, that she played old-fashioned pursuits with Jimmy, from cards to board games. It allowed them both a small escape, and it pleased her to see a single, childless Jimmy able to revisit his youth with her, to relive more innocent times. Angie may have only been thirteen, but it had been long enough for the world to kick her ass several times. As a result, she was wiser than many people gave her credit for, her family included.

Jimmy occasionally fell into that trap, but more often than not, he respected her intelligence and never deliberately patronized her. Maybe it was because she was the baby of the family by some margin. Still, he had always treated her differently. Angie felt that she enjoyed a special relationship with Jimmy, one of mutual understanding. It was because of this that she knew he was now genuinely worried. He had tried to disguise it, but Jimmy had been glancing at the clock mounted on the wall behind her with increased regularity. Something was wrong.

They both focused in the direction of the warehouse's main entrance, just to the office's side, as a sharp crack was heard. The entryway comprised two huge wooden doors that swung inwards to allow vehicles through, but built into the left one was a standard-sized door for foot traffic only. It was this door that had been booted open and had slammed hard against the larger wooden portal it was part off, sending a crack echoing through the warehouse. Before that echo had even dissipated, the yelling started.

'Jimmy, get out here now!' came a female voice, thick with a Brooklyn accent.

Jimmy and Angie bolted up from their chairs and dashed out of the office. As soon as she saw the trio of new arrivals, Angie had to fight the urge to burst into tears. Being supported on either side, her arms wrapped around the other two, was Angie's oldest sister, Cassidy Archer. Even against the black of her jumpsuit, the sizeable glossy patch of crimson near her left shoulder was evident. Parts of her blonde hair were matted with blood, and her eyes were barely open as she struggled to walk, almost drunk in appearance.

Delilah Archer, propping up Cassidy from the left, was the second oldest, just a year younger. A short-haired brunette, Delilah was slightly shorter than Cassidy but far more toned, her jumpsuit concealing a physique sculpted by hundreds of hours spent at the gym expending the aggressive energy that was natural to her. A darkish-red and purple ring had started to form around her left eye, inflicted by a blow from something or someone.

Underneath Cassidy's right arm was Bethany Archer. She was two years younger than Delilah and previously the baby of the family, until Angie's appearance twelve years later, a 'pleasant surprise' as her parents had admitted. The aura of confidence and self-assurance bordering on arrogance that defined the beautiful Bethany was seemingly buckling just as much as her body, struggling as it was to carry both her assault rifle and an increasingly limp Cassidy.

Bethany looked at a frozen Jimmy in desperation.

'She's hit!' she blurted breathlessly.

The bullet slams into the area just below Cassidy's left shoulder. It sends her flying back as if punched by a boxer, an arc of blood trailing in the air as she descends. She hits the gravel hard, and for a moment, all she can see through the eyes of the Wolfman mask are the dull grey skies of New York in October. She then feels gloved fingers slide down the back of her neck and her collar tightens before she is dragged along the ground and deposited behind a car. All the while, she hears gunfire around her, a ceaseless cacophony. She looks up to see Dracula - her father, Axel - and Frankenstein - Delilah - unleashing a torrent of bullets, while a recovered Witch - Bethany - gently props Cassidy up against the car door.

While Delilah maintains fire, Axel throws his backpack to the ground, reaches into the top compartment, and pulls out three cylindrical smoke grenades. He pulls the pins and tosses them short, medium, and long distances. Within seconds thick grey smoke starts to disperse around the area, but it does not stop the incoming fire as more car windows explode around them. The one above Cassidy's head shatters, showering her with small crystalline pellets.

'Get her in the office, now!' declared Jimmy authoritatively, the years of training instantly reasserting themselves.

Delilah and Bethany followed him, dragging Cassidy into the office, her boot tips scraping the floor as they went. Jimmy swept his arms across the desk and knocked all the assorted paraphernalia to the floor. He did not have to say a word, as the two sisters laid Cassidy on the wooden surface as gently as they could. Jimmy opened the top drawer of one of the nearby filing cabinets and pulled out an extensive first aid case and a small cool box. He placed them down on free spaces next to Cassidy's head and opened them. Out of the cool box, he pulled two bags, one of saline and the other blood with 'Cassidy' written in thick black marker across it. The cool box contents were always kept ready on such days, just in case, yet another backup on which Axel insisted, on this occasion wisely.

'We tried stopping the bleeding, but she's lost a lot,' reported Bethany. 'No exit wound either.'

Jimmy gently tapped Cassidy's cheek as she groaned.

'Cass, come on hun, stay awake. It's okay, you're safe now, we'll get you patched up,' he said with a tone of reassuring conviction.

As Jimmy pulled on a pair of surgical gloves and retrieved some substantial scissors from the first aid case, Angie, standing in the doorway, could only look on at the scene as if it were a movie playing out before her. It was the ultimate immersive experience that she couldn't switch off. The macabre spectacle caused Angie to want to look away, run away even, but compelled her to keep her eyes fixed on Cassidy as she started to writhe around in pain as Jimmy cut away at the patch of jumpsuit near her wound.

'What happened?' croaked Angie.

'A total fuckin' shit show is what happened!' raged Delilah as she pounded a fist against a nearby plywood wall.

'Hey!' barked Jimmy. 'Not the time, Dee. Come over and help me.'

Delilah moved towards Jimmy, her hand outstretched to take the blood bag he offered. The movement caught Cassidy's attention, her alertness raised slightly as more blood flowed to her head now that she was flat. Her eyes widened, and her lips suddenly curled into a vicious snarl.

'Get away from me, you crazy bitch!' screamed Cassidy as she lashed out, the intense rage she felt poorly conveyed through weak arms that barely contacted Delilah's chest. 'It's all your fault!'

Jimmy, taken aback for a second, regained his composure and quickly took control of Cassidy's arms, gently pressing them back onto the table.

'Calm yourself, girl,' he whispered soothingly, his face only inches from hers.

'Where's Dad?'

It was a question that caused everyone to turn their gaze towards Angie, who stood silently in the doorway, pinching a couple of the buttons of her denim jacket, waiting for an answer. Jimmy glanced towards Bethany, who started to tear up and shake her head.

Cassidy looks up to Axel, and though she cannot see his face, his body language speaks volumes. His knuckles support his balance as he rests on one knee while his head is bowed, as if in prayer. She only looks on for a few seconds, but it seems to stretch to eternity for Cassidy. Her father is wilting before her eyes. It is one thing to face mounting, even hopeless odds with comrades in arms around you. But your own flesh and blood?

Axel angles himself forwards and brings his head close to hers. He has to shout to make himself heard above the din and through the muffling of the masks.

'There's no way this ends well, kiddo, and so remember, if there's no way out-'

Axel rips off his Dracula mask and shoves it into Cassidy's free hand.

'Make your own.'

Cassidy instantly knows what is coming. So does Bethany, sitting adjacent to her. They both reach out simultaneously, but it is too late. Axel has already risen, dropped his rifle, and has started sprinting into the smoke. Delilah pauses her firing, the Frankenstein mask tilting slightly in bemusement before she snaps her gaze to her sisters as realization hits.

All three scream after Axel, but as Cassidy manages to haul herself up to get a look, all she sees is their father falling to his knees and bellowing his surrender as he raises his arms and opens his hands wide.

Cassidy keeps her eyes on him for as long as she can, screaming for him almost continuously even as Delilah and Bethany pull her away. Her last image of Axel is the temporarily disturbed smoke he has left in his wake swirling back to fill the void and envelop him as the ESU team's dark silhouettes rapidly move in and encircle.

Jimmy swallowed hard.

'Angie, honey,' he said, trying to keep an even tone in his voice. 'I need you and Dee to head to the back and open up that crate I showed you a while ago. There are some bags inside. Start getting them ready.'

'But-' began Angie at the exact same time as an incredulous Delilah barked, 'I ain't fuckin' goin' nowhere!'

'Now!' hissed Jimmy, shutting down any argument from both parties.

A chastened Delilah bowed her head. After a moment's hesitation, she quickly moved to the doorway and gently guided Angie away from the office and towards the rear of the warehouse. Jimmy reached into the first aid case and tossed Bethany a pair of surgical gloves.

'You're assisting, Beth. You remember what I taught you, right?'

Bethany shook her head, sniffling. Jimmy smiled gently.

'You will.'

He looked down at Cassidy and stroked her hair.

'Cass, I'm gonna give you something for the pain, but I gotta get that bullet out, and it's gonna sting like a son of a bitch.'

'Dad said getting shot hurt like nothing he ever knew,' she replied. 'I never really believed him until now. Oh, Jesus…'

Cassidy's lower lip started to quiver. Her eyes watered up as memories less than an hour old forced themselves through the pain and into her mind's eye. Jimmy hushed her and discreetly reached for the surgical tongs in the first aid case.

Even at the far end of the warehouse, the sound was clear. Delilah hugged Angie tight as the young girl shuddered at the piercing screams.

***

Cassidy stood in front of the railing that prevented her from falling into the Hudson River. She was tempted to vault it and let the murky waters claim her and all her problems. It would have been easy enough, for it had only been a few hours since her impromptu surgery. Cassidy was barely in a condition to walk, let alone swim.

Her left arm was in a sling, the thick layer of gauze and bandages that covered her shoulder wound concealed by a leather jacket. Cassidy should have been resting, at least for a few days. Jimmy had insisted on it, but she had dismissed his concerns, opting instead to be dosed up with antibiotics and painkillers. Time was of the essence. She and the others had to get out of the city as soon as possible. It was also likely that the NYPD would pay Jimmy a visit as a known associate of the recently captured Axel Archer. The wheels had started turning as soon as her father had surrendered. Nothing would stop them now, so what was the point of delaying? The Archer sisters needed to move. A bed in some anonymous hotel was as good as any.

The worst of Cassidy's nausea, resulting from too much medication and not enough food, had passed. Still, she occasionally caught herself tasting bile in her throat. She ignored it despite the bitter taste in her mouth, though perhaps that was just her growing rage at the day's injustice manifesting itself. Her life as she had known it was over, snatched away in an instant. But those were the breaks. At least she would be able to walk away, unlike her father.

Nevertheless, Cassidy would miss the city. The reflected skyline of Lower Manhattan filled her shades as she gazed across the water. On the occasional quiet day, she would come to the very spot she stood on to take in the view and its majesty. That was why they were all present now, to capture a final mental snapshot in case they never saw it again. Brooklyn was home and in the sisters' blood, but Lady Liberty, Ellis Island, even where the Twin Towers had once stood, and a new single tower dominated, were part of the city's story. As New Yorkers, the Archer girls were part of that story too, like eight million others. That would never change, even if their names had to.

Cassidy turned around to face the others. A few hundred yards away was the Central Railroad of New Jersey Terminal. The red brick and dark slate-roofed building had an almost gothic church-like quality to it, aided by the clock tower that emerged from the center of the enormous rectangular structure. Formerly the waterfront passenger terminal of Jersey City, it was now a railroad museum. Upon their arrival, it had conveniently allowed Jimmy and the sisters to blend in amidst the groups of visitors. Seeking some quiet, they had retreated to the south-east corner of Liberty Park, with its view of Ellis Island across the water to the right and Lower Manhattan straight ahead. They were in Hoboken, New Jersey, no longer in New York State. It was as fitting a place as any, thought Cassidy. Whether by road or rail, who knew which states they would end up in? America was getting smaller all the time but was still just about big enough to get lost in, or so she hoped.

Cassidy cricked her neck. To her left stood Angie, also pretending to look out across the water. Even though fifteen years separated them, Angie and Cassidy looked so similar that they could have been twins had the years balanced out. Tall and athletic with long blonde hair and angular faces, both had clearly taken after their mother. In contrast, Delilah and Bethany had inherited their father's dark hair and square-faced genes. What Cassidy had inherited from her father was Axel's steely determination and laser-like focus on a task. An arch strategist, her calm manner and cool detachment were often mistaken for iciness, for lack of emotion. Still, those closest to her knew that she was as emotional and passionate as anyone, just better at hiding it, to retain a degree of mystery. Not for Cassidy was heart to be worn on the sleeve. Everyone knew that was the preserve of the fiery and passionate Delilah.

Further down from the group was the girl herself, her back to the railing, ever the rebel. In contrast to Cassidy and Angie's pale blue ones, Delilah's eyes were a deep brown, dark, almost to the point of blending into the pupils. Angie had sometimes discreetly commented to Cassidy that she felt Delilah's eyes to be kind of fitting, for she sensed inner darkness in their sister, buried deep but gradually making its way to the surface in recent years. Cassidy had found it hard to challenge the young girl's perception and had likewise felt a growing sense of danger around her sister, like wariness of a beloved dog starting to show signs of increased aggression. Delilah had finally bitten, in the bank, and it had been too late to put a muzzle on her. Now, only hours after the score from hell, Delilah stood but a few yards away, yet she may as well have been on the opposite bank of the Hudson, such was the emotional gulf apparent between her and Cassidy.

Bethany, standing between them with Angie at her side, could feel the tension cut through her each way like invisible arrows. By far, Bethany was the prettiest of the four, possessing an hourglass figure, kind face, and warm eyes that had drawn male attention since high school and beyond. While she was not unaware of her looks, she prioritized her creativity and intellect. Though life had stubbornly ignored her artistic dreams, Bethany had still found some outlet in the family 'business' through assuming a range of disguises and identities to scope out or infiltrate prospective targets. Now, she sensed, she would need to exploit all of those skills to remain a free woman long enough to start painting the blank canvas she knew her life was about to become.

Jimmy stood to Cassidy's right, quietly lost in his own thoughts. Even though he had quickly found out what had happened at the bank, he had not passed judgment or had not seemed to at least. Perhaps Jimmy's blood was boiling that his friend of over thirty years was languishing in police custody, that Axel's face was already appearing on websites and social media feeds, would no doubt lead the local news bulletins, and be plastered across the morning newspapers. If that were the case, though, then it was impossible to tell. Jimmy was certainly not blasé, but nor was he a well of emotions. Maybe it would come out later in private, but not here, not now, not with work to be done and his team to extract from danger, not least before the police caught up with him for questioning. It was the mark of a true professional, thought Cassidy.

Plain black rucksacks, one for each sister, rested on the ground next to her, Bethany and Delilah. Angie had no bag. Neither did Jimmy. He sighed heavily and turned to them.

'The cops have Axel. Nothing we can do about that, but at least he's alive. Now we just gotta follow the plan we put in place if something like this ever happened. In your go-bags, you'll each find your new lives. Passports, social security numbers, clean bank accounts, and a little money to get you by until I can start regular transfers from the fund.'

'How long are we talkin' here?' probed Bethany.

'Hard to say,' replied Jimmy with a brief shrug. 'We need space, and you need to get yourselves lost. That's why each pack also has a burner phone. I'm the only one who has the numbers. They're for me to contact you guys, or for you to reach me in an emergency. Nothing else. As for when you can come back? It could be weeks, months-'

'Years,' stated Bethany flatly.

Jimmy could only respond with a silent nod. Suddenly Angie slapped the railing with her palms and looked up at the sky, her frustration evident.

'This is *such* bullshit! We're just leavin' it all behind? This isn't a shitty couch dumped in a back alley, this is our lives we're walkin' away from here. And what the hell about Dad?'

'It's hard, honey. I know, believe me,' said Jimmy soothingly. 'But the cops are sweatin' him right now. We need to put distance between you guys and him. He was black and white about that if he was ever captured.'

'Dad won't break. He'd never give us up!' protested Angie.

'This ain't some tin-pot dictatorship. They ain't gonna torture or break him,' said Jimmy, his tone starting to harden. 'But all it can take is one slip, a tiny one, a loose word or a look in his eyes and they'll know they have somethin' to go on. And even if he didn't give 'em anything, after the clusterfu-' He caught his language, paused a second and continued. 'After the mess at the bank, it'll take the NYPD all of five seconds to make the link between a female crew and that Axel has daughters, if they haven't put two and two together already. I wouldn't be surprised if they were kickin' down your door right now, warrant in hand and questions on lips. My warehouse will sure as hell be on their list.'

Angie gripped the railing hard with both hands and squeezed her eyes shut in frustration.

'But there's gotta be *somethin'* we can do.'

She opened her eyes as they started to tear up. She turned left to Bethany, who could only look down to the ground as she struggled to contain her own emotions. Angie turned right to Cassidy, only to find her oldest sister continuing to stare across the Hudson, betraying nothing. All the young girl could do was lower her own head, resigned to helplessness.

'I say we bust him out,' said Delilah out of nowhere. She stepped away from the railing and approached the group. 'Dad would be ripping the place apart if it was one of us in a cell.'

Jimmy stepped towards her, shaking his head, his anger starting to boil up. Why didn't she suggest taking down the Federal Reserve while they were at it?

'Bust him out? What the hell are you talkin' about! There's no Hollywood ending here, ladies! There are no daring rescues, leaping from helicopters, jumping bridges in sports cars. This is the name of the game. We can win, and we can lose. This is what losing looks like. Fuckin' deal with it!'

Jimmy closed his eyes and bit his lower lip, silently chastising himself for his aggression. He should have been more understanding, especially with Angie around. But he couldn't entertain stupidity either.

Delilah's own temper was starting to flare, her tone laced with ice as she tried to suppress the fire rising inside her.

'I hear what you're sayin' Jimmy, but I ain't just standin' around with my thumb stuck up my ass. I'm not just gonna pack a bag, hitch a ride and-'

'Leave? Yeah, Dee, that's exactly what you're gonna do. All of you,' interjected Jimmy. 'Don't think for a second Axel wouldn't do the same. He was a professional, and yeah, it woulda tore him up, tore him up bad, but he'd of walked, no hesitations, especially if it meant sacrificing one of you to keep the others safe. He had to do it in the Service plenty of times.'

'This ain't fuckin' Delta Force, Jimmy, this is family!' barked Delilah. 'Fuck your code, fuck your professionalism. Blood is thicker than all that.'

Cassidy sighed and stepped back from the railing. She continued to gaze out across the water as she spoke, her tone neutral.

'Jimmy's right. It's time for us to go.'

Delilah shot her an incredulous look that veered towards disgust.

'Oh, that's it then. End of debate. Cassidy has spoken.'

Cassidy turned to Delilah and removed her shades. Bethany, who had looked up from the ground to witness the unfolding argument, swallowed hard. She was taken aback by the look in Cassidy's eyes, not because they were filled with frustration, anger, hate, or loathing. No. It was because Cassidy's eyes showed no feeling at all, such was her contempt.

'You have no right to speak at all after what you did,' said Cassidy calmly and coldly. 'You've destroyed everything. You're not even a fuck-up. You're less than that. You're a straight nothing and always will be.'

It was a deliberate icicle to the heart. Jimmy stepped forwards and raised a hand.

'Whoa Cass, easy there.'

But Cassidy wasn't listening. She could tell from Delilah's reaction that she had wounded her. Now she wanted to finish the job.

'Whatever happens to Dad, you've already killed him.'

Delilah's face started to scrunch up as she tried to hold back the tears, unsuccessfully.

'Fuck you, Cass, fuck you!' she exploded in a burst of rage and hurt.

She locked stares with Cassidy, both of them silent. Delilah looked away first, flinching under Cassidy's uncompromising gaze. She glanced towards Bethany and Angie, who could only look away out of shame and pity. Jimmy was the only one who considered her with sympathy, but he too remained silent. It spoke volumes to Delilah. She wiped a sleeve across her nose and shook her head, her lips quivering.

'Go to hell, all of you,' she whispered with a dismissive wave of her hand.

Delilah turned on her heel, grabbed her nearby go-bag, and started marching off towards the Terminal building. Bethany clutched her chest as she watched her go.

'Please, Dee, don't leave like this!' she called out.

'Let her go. There's nothing more to say,' said Cassidy impatiently.

Silently, she slid her shades back on, stepped over to Bethany, and hugged her tightly with her good arm. She took a side step, did the same to Angie, then turned to

Jimmy. She stepped towards him, but he took the initiative and wrapped his huge arms around her, holding her a moment, careful of her shoulder. Bethany knew that Cassidy was the epitome of self-control. However, she was still convinced that she heard the subtlest of sniffling from her usually cool sister. Jimmy finally released Cassidy. Without a word, she grabbed her own go-bag and marched off in the opposite direction to Delilah, heading south-west along the waterline.

'How can she just leave that easily?' demanded Angie bitterly. 'She didn't even look back at us.'

Bethany wiped away a tear and leaned in to hug Angie.

'No honey,' she whispered into Angie's ear. 'If she looked back, then she might never leave, and leaving us is the hardest thing she's ever had to do.'

Bethany kissed Angie's cheek, stepped back, and grabbed her bag from the ground. A saddened Jimmy took her in his arms a moment before she pulled back, cast a last mournful look at him and Angie, and turned away, her direction also the Terminal building.

Jimmy and Angie stood alone as they watched her vanish into the crowds milling around the building entrance. He put a gentle hand on Angie's shoulder. She looked up to him.

'What about me?'

***

Jimmy pulled up to the main entrance of the old mansion. Its original Nineteenth Century ornate sandstone architecture was extended by two modern-day but complementary wings that stretched off a few hundred yards in each direction. The front of the complex concealed a large estate that contained a variety of smaller buildings, water features, sports fields, and immaculately tended lawns and gardens, all of which were encircled by a thick line of trees. They were in the countryside now, the New York City skyline just about visible on the distant horizon. For Angie, though, they may as well have been on Mars.

After they had seen off her sisters, Jimmy had driven them not to Brooklyn, but to Manhattan. He had deposited Angie at an expensive-looking salon, where he had politely requested that an effeminate but friendly male hairdresser transform the untidy length of blonde hair that ran halfway down her back into something far more stylish and manageable. Jimmy had then disappeared. Angie had waited for a couple of hours, first bored then increasingly concerned, until just as suddenly Jimmy reappeared wearing a suit and holding what looked like a school uniform. It was a dark blue blazer and tie, white shirt, light blue skirt, white stockings, and low black heels. Despite her questions, which quickly led to protestations after they failed to be answered, Jimmy first encouraged then demanded that she dress in the uniform.

Angie had retreated to a changing room and did as she was told. She had taken a moment to consider herself in the mirror. Who was the stranger that stared back at her, with her now silky neck-length hair and smart, pressed uniform? Jimmy had then led her out onto the street, where instead of his usual SUV, she found a silver Bentley Continental waiting. Jimmy had quickly ushered her into the back seat, brushing off her pleas for information with promises that answers would soon come.

Angie knew Jimmy well enough not to keep poking him. If he had not immediately answered her questions, he had his reasons, even if she had grown increasingly frustrated at her enforced ignorance. All she could do was run a finger over the emblem sewn onto her blazer's left breast. It was the shape of a medieval shield, upon which a fountain pen and old-style quill were crossed with each other above an open book. An eagle was perched upon the crossed writing implements, its wings spread wide. The motto beneath the shield was written in Latin, but Angie used her phone to translate it. *Let learning take flight*, it read. Now, parked outside the mansion, it all made sense.

'This is a school, Jimmy,' she observed, her face pressed against the window.

'That it is,' he replied. 'Harrington Academy, where kids come for the finest education money can buy. Stolen or otherwise.' He turned around in his seat. 'This'll be home now.'

Angie slowly shook her head in disbelief.

'No, Jimmy, come on! I know we gotta lay low, but this is crazy. This ain't me! I'm just a kid from Brooklyn. My family robs banks, not owns them!'

'What do you think most of that money was for, Angie?'

'Cut the crap,' she replied irritably. 'We both know that Dad and the girls got off on this shit, it wasn't just about buyin' me a better future.'

'Hey, watch your language. Kids here don't talk like that.'

'I ain't nothin' like kids here.'

'Then play the part. This was always gonna happen. Your Dad was gonna send you to a prep school before college. Events just sped things up a little is all.'

'No shit. What, you pull this Bentley out your ass?'

'I had to make a few calls to the admissions board, make a reasonable donation, borrow the right car, buy the right suit for me, and whatever the hell rich girls your age wear for you,' acknowledged Jimmy with a shrug. 'Gotta paint a picture. You're Angelina Fairchild, only daughter of a Wall Street power couple who had to transfer to Singapore last minute, but who wanted you to stay in the US.'

'And who are you, my butler?' asked Angie acidly.

Jimmy frowned.

'The kids here are on vacation for a few weeks, just a skeleton staff on campus. It'll give you time to settle in, get a feel for the place, work on your character. I got everything you need in the trunk. New clothes, phone, laptop.'

'It'll take me five minutes to set up a fake life online for whoever it is I'm supposed to be,' huffed Angie. 'What won't take five minutes is knowin' how to live that life.'

'Just watch *My Fair Lady*,' muttered Jimmy, half to himself. He shook his head. 'Look, Angie, honey, this ain't gonna be easy. I never said it would be. And I'm sorry it's gotta be this way. You don't think I'd rather have you stay with me? Every day, no question. But the cops'll be watching me, and I don't want 'em watching you too. But you know how I can do this, even though it hurts? It's because I know you can handle it. I know you're strong. I know that you're more than just what people see in front of 'em, even your Dad and sisters sometimes. I believe in you, Angie Archer.'

Jimmy's speech was heartfelt, and Angie knew it. She felt a lump grow in her throat as the anger and resentment she felt temporarily dissipated. Things had happened so fast since their morning card games that Angie had barely been able to process them. She instinctively knew that tears would flow freely that evening when she was alone and afraid, in a strange place, in the dark, the devils of her mind free to dance. The enormity of what was happening to her had only just begun to sink in. She would have to digest it in bitesize portions. It would be the only way to avoid the whole situation overwhelming her. But she was sure of one thing. Her old life was now over, gone. Whatever the new one held for her, nothing would ever be the same again, and she would have to face it alone. The tears might come later, but from that moment, she promised herself that no one else would ever see them again.

She wiped away a tear forming in her eye before it could roll down her cheek and affect the makeup the salon had applied. She looked away briefly and cleared her throat before locking eyes with Jimmy once again.

'Don't you mean Angelina Fairchild?'

FIVE YEARS LATER

1

Cassidy stepped out onto the porch of her cabin and gently blew on her steaming cup of coffee. It was a morning ritual she had observed since buying the place almost a year ago, a hidden retreat in the Appalachian Mountains of West Virginia. It had been a cash-in-hand deal, a quick exchange of money for the deed, and no questions. In return, she had access to a stunning view of forests, distant mountains, and a spiderweb of walking trails that surrounded the rustic wooden cabin and the small clearing in front of it. A poorly-maintained barbed wire fence ringed the perimeter of the few acres she owned, the occasional faded 'No Trespassing' sign signaling to strangers and neighbors - not that she had any - that all were equally unwelcome.

Cassidy had cleaned out the inside of the old cabin, renovated it as best she could, and had installed a few modern conveniences. Otherwise, she was off the grid, and that was how she liked it. Apart from a burner phone - separate to the one Jimmy had given her, which was stashed in a drawer in her bedroom, never used once - her only connection to the outside world was a battered but reliable pickup truck she had bought from a used-car dealership, its white paint job gradually losing the fight against growing rust spots.

While Cassidy periodically wandered into the nearby town to stock up on supplies, grab a drink at the bar, or even catch a movie, she seldom left her retreat. She had what could be considered acquaintances, people at the bar or the local store she would greet and engage in mildly diverting small talk, but she did not have friends. Her passport said Cassidy Monroe, but she had always simply identified by her first name. At least that had been something Jimmy had allowed each sister to keep from their past life.

Not that she had actually changed that much if she was honest with herself. Perhaps her sisters had become entirely different people in their new lives. Cassidy had no idea, but she had stubbornly refused to change. She had always been quiet and cautious, her contemplative nature often mistaken for aloofness. Cassidy would happily talk in small groups of three or four during her school days but shrink into herself when surrounded by more, content to sit back and study others, take in information, and process what to do with it. She was, above all, a thinker, capable of delivering on a plan with single-minded determination. Perhaps that was why she had clicked so well with her father's criminal life, even if the early days of the sisters' involvement in the crew had been borne out of necessity in trying to save their mother rather than indulge in outlaw greed or immature thrill-seeking.

Back in Virginia, Cassidy was just outgoing enough not to be considered some weird recluse, perhaps meriting suspicion, but nor was she so sociable that people would start wondering what her story was, where she had come from, what she was doing up in the cabin alone. Better she cultivated the mystery as to whether she was an artist or a writer who needed space and quiet, as opposed to some crazy woman who locked children up in her basement.

No doubt, the stereotypical image in people's minds would be one where she was surrounded by cats, but the only company she actually kept was a husky called Riley, a stray she had adopted from a regional dog shelter. Despite his size, Riley was relaxed and gentle, more likely to jump up on a stranger and slobber over them than savage. He lay on the porch, lazily bathing in the warm morning sun. Cassidy smiled and shook her head.

'Get your ass up, you need some exercise.'

She downed the rest of her coffee, set the cup aside on a nearby window frame, and cricked her neck.

'But first, I need mine.'

***

Cassidy stood at the mouth of the dirt track that ran through the dense woodland. She was dressed in black Lycra jogging pants and top and wore dusty running shoes. Several throwing knives were sleeved in the wide brown-leather belt that looped around her waist. In her right hand, she held a semi-automatic pistol with a silencer attached. A watch looped around her left wrist that she had set to stopwatch mode. She closed her eyes, breathed deeply, exhaled gently, and tapped a side button to start the clock.

Cassidy instantly launched into a sprint down the winding dirt path. As she ran, she deliberately hit several thin tripwires she had set up the day before. As each wire broke, an empty tin can attached to a string dropped down several feet from a nearby tree branch, each can already pocked with numerous holes. As Cassidy passed one, she would aim while moving and plant a silenced round in it, a metallic ding signaling a confirmed hit. Each can became progressively smaller in size, increasing the difficulty of the shot. Still, she managed to bullseye every one of them with ease. Cassidy made a mental note to change locations and further reduce their sizes when she reset the course for another run. It was becoming too intuitive, too easy to remember, lacking in surprise. It would not do.

Cassidy cleared half a dozen target cans and came upon the midpoint marker of her improvised assault course. It was the first of several large fallen tree branches that she had dragged onto the path at irregular intervals. She dropped her pistol onto some obvious scrub for later retrieval and launched into a dive over the first branch, positioned at waist-height. Cassidy finessed her angle as she flew and landed into a seamless roll. She used the forward momentum to get to her feet and carry on running. She repeated this maneuver three more times, the branches progressively increasing in height. On the final leap, she felt one of the small sharp twig stumps that lined the branch scratch her midriff, throwing her off enough that her flow was interrupted. She landed with an awkward roll, slowing her pace considerably. She grimaced, but at least there was no need to adjust the difficulty of the branch leaps.

Cassidy sprinted a dozen more yards, skidded to a stop on the dry dirt, and found the first target to her left, a basic rectangular plywood board nailed to a tree. She had glued on a target practice sheet procured from a local shooting range, the standard black silhouette of a human target with scoring rings laid over it. Cassidy quickly drew one of the throwing knives from her belt and flung it at the target. The blade buried itself deep into what would have been the forehead of a real person.

She looked ahead of her and spotted the second board, the same as the first but slightly further away. She drew another knife, threw it, and achieved the same result. She then turned to her right, spotted the third and final target board, and threw her last remaining knife. Whether it was the slightly elevated angle as a result of the board being placed on a slope, or the deliberately challenging distance she had set it at, the knife failed to land on the black silhouette itself, planting its blade in the light brown area of the paper surface, an inch away from the head but a miss nonetheless. It was an automatic five second penalty.

Sweating and breathless, Cassidy stopped the timer and glanced at the result. She squeezed her eyes shut and cursed loudly. Not good enough. Too slow. Far too slow.

***

Cassidy heard Riley barking before she saw him. She approached the clearing in front of her cabin with caution and noted a strange SUV parked nearby. She relaxed when she saw who had sparked such excitement in the dog, who eagerly chased after a stick thrown long and far. Cole Samson turned towards the path from which Cassidy emerged and raised a broad smile, the beam of his pearly whites as irresistible as ever. A tall and muscular African-American with a shaved head and neatly trimmed beard, Cole had a strong physical presence but carried an easy charm and was blessed with a keen intellect. Depending on the clothing he wore, he could either be taken for a heavyweight boxer or a college professor. He was also one of the finest thieves Cassidy had ever met.

She approached him with her own smile and they embraced warmly. There was no romantic undercurrent. They were firm friends only and always would be. Indeed, some of the risky scores and close escapes they had experienced had arguably bonded them far more than any romance could have. After leaving New York, Cassidy had eventually found herself in Los Angeles, one of the biggest bank and armored car robbery towns in America. After two years, the heat had started to become too much, and so Cassidy had returned to the East Coast. She had skipped over New York and headed for Boston, where her West Coast contacts had put her in touch with Cole. The rest was history.

For two years, they had developed their partnership of successful jobs, often favoring stealth, subtlety, and more thoughtful approaches to thievery than the brute force smash and grabs typical of Los Angeles. After being hired to steal information from a powerful law firm, Cassidy had finally realized that, as single-minded and dedicated as she was, even she was approaching burnout. She had thrown a dart at a map to let fate determine her escape and ended up in West Virginia. She had not abandoned Cole, though, and had offered him sanctuary whenever he needed it. Given that he had never visited her before, and West Virginia was far enough away from Massachusetts to rule out a simple social call, his presence could only mean that such sanctuary was now required.

Riley came bounding back and dropped the saliva-covered stick at Cassidy's feet.

'You got one hell of a guard dog there,' observed Cole casually, as if it had only been days since their last encounter. 'What does he do with intruders? Kill 'em with kindness?'

'Riley's a good judge of character. If he thought you were gonna hurt me, it'd probably be your balls he dropped at my feet, not a stick.'

'That so, huh?'

'You okay?' she probed.

'Yeah, course,' he nodded absentmindedly, his attention still captured by Riley's whining pleas to throw more sticks. He relented, threw another long one, and turned to Cassidy. 'I just needed to get out of Boston for a while, change of scene. I was feeling the heat a little, you know? Thought I'd come check on you. It's been too long, Cass.'

'That it has,' she acknowledged with a sigh. 'Well, you missed breakfast, but I figure the occasion calls for mixing up some more pancake batter.'

'You know the way to this boy's heart,' responded Cole with a satisfied nod. 'But what I really wanna know is if you still be mixing the Cassidy Special?'

'Guess you'll have to wait until sundown to find out,' replied Cassidy with a playful wink as she headed into the cabin.

Cole chuckled at her teasing and followed. He kept a few steps back and slowed his pace. Unseen by Cassidy, his smile faded, and a severe expression took over. His leisurely advance bought him just enough time to perform a slow three-sixty rotation before he reached the porch, subtly rechecking their surroundings to confirm they were alone.

2

The motel room was musky, pervaded by the combined scent of sweat and sex. The strong beams of the morning Nevada sun half-penetrated the thin, worn curtains, highlighting the dust that swirled in the air. The yellow of the beams complemented the drab orange of the room's painted walls and light browns of the ancient furniture fabric. A plume of cigarette smoke swirled into the light. The no-smoking sign on the wall had long been covered by a faded sticker of a marijuana leaf, and in any case, the smoke alarm seemed to be broken. Most of the rooms belonging to the roadside motel were in the same condition. Even in the Seventies, the decor would have been considered dated. Still, it was suitably cheap and, most importantly to many of its clients, out of the way.

Delilah sat on the end of the creaky double bed, dressed only in black underwear and a white vest top. She stared into space and occasionally sucked on the cigarette that smoldered between her fingers, small clumps of ash dropping onto the matted carpet. Five years had seen her physique become even leaner and toned. Nothing grotesque, just well-defined biceps, calves, and abs. She had grown her dark hair to shoulder-length, and several years spent in the American Southwest had given her skin a healthy tan. She had exercised away most of her natural breasts long ago and, because she was fond of them, had bought new ones. Nothing slutty, just the right size, like the dress and heels that rested upon the cracked leather armchair across the room.

In addition to a more defined musculature, she had added a collection of tattoos. They were an assortment of small and medium-sized creatures, symbols, and words dotted across her upper arms and back. Most were inked on her because she thought they looked cool, some because she had been beyond drunk and had no idea what her motivations had been at the time. The sole tattoo that held any meaning to her, which she sometimes rubbed without realizing it, was a stylized black bow and arrow on her upper left arm, an exact replica of her father's one. It was a reminder to herself that the Delilah Taylor of her passport and driving license was, and would always be, Delilah Archer, laying low be damned.

Delilah sits on the steps of the Archer house, pressing a soda can against her right eye. The cool moisture on its surface feels good, helping ease the burn of what is sure to be an impressive shiner come the next morning. She pulls the ring off the can and gulps down the surgery liquid. She doesn't notice as Axel quietly sits down beside her. His sudden appearance causes her to jump slightly, coughing and spluttering as she does.

'Jesus fucking Christ, Dad!'

'You watch your mouth young lady,' responds Axel, his volume measured but the tone unmistakably hard.

Delilah looks down at her feet, suitably chastised.

'Yes sir,' she replies sheepishly.

After a moment's silence to ensure his authority is established, Axel continues, his tone deliberately softer. He knows exactly which track to take when handling Delilah.

'You want to tell me what happened?' he probes, staring out onto the street and the passersby.

'I'm pretty sure you'll get the full picture from Cass, she saw it all. Hell, that's all she does is see. Just watches and thinks. Strange girl. Did we ever get her checked out?'

'Stop dancing Dee and answer the question, straight.'

'Mark Bridges called you a baby-killing war criminal, so I knocked out his front teeth. Then his two buddies took a shot,' she recounted, pointing at her rapidly bruising eye. 'So I broke one guy's nose and rammed my knee into the other one's balls, made him puke. That straight enough for you?'

Axel sighs and rubs his eyes with a thumb and forefinger.

'Jesus, Dee.'

'I know I disappoint you, that Cass is your favorite,' says Delilah matter-of-factly as she finishes the soda and scrunches the middle of the can.

'I don't have a favorite. You're all different, and that's what I love about you.'

'Yeah, I've always been the most trouble,' says Delilah with a half chuckle.

'Truth be told, you're right,' acknowledges Axel.

Delilah inhales sharply. It's not the response she was expecting, convinced that he would try and bat away the assertion and placate her.

'But you want to know another truth?' continues Axel. 'It's because of that that you're probably the one who's most like me.'

Axel breaks away from gazing upon the street and locks eyes with Delilah, leaving her in no doubt that he's being honest.

'If there was trouble in this borough, either I went lookin' for it, or it came to me. God, I had such a fire in me until the army helped cool it, just enough anyway. Your mom helped with the rest. Now, kiddo, you've got the fire in you too. Nothing like Cass or Beth. But you gotta learn to control it. Otherwise, one day, it'll burn your insides right up. I don't care what people think or say I did on operations, and neither should you. And you sure as hell

shouldn't use the training I've been giving you all to lash out. That's to defend yourself, not for breaking teeth.'

'They had it coming,' protests Delilah. 'Sometimes the world just needs its ass kicked.'

'Maybe so,' replies Axel soothingly rather than risk an argument. 'But there are times in life you just gotta know when to pull the trigger and when not to. I can help a little with that, but ultimately it's your finger. Still, if a young punk like me can end up serving his country and marrying an angel, then there's hope for you yet, Delilah Archer.'

Axel follows this up with a wink and a gentle smile. He hopes he has said enough, at least to stop her spiraling, but he knows it will be a continuing battle for the next few all-important formative years.

'You really think I'm most like you?' she asks him earnestly.

'God, I hope not,' he chuckles. 'I sucked at school. At least you've not been kicked out.'

'Yet,' retorts Delilah.

'Well, your mom and I will go see the principal tomorrow, try and smooth things over as best we can. Those boys will look as bad or worse for beating on a girl.'

'That's nothing. Half the school watched a twelve-year-old beat the crap out of three guys two years older. They'll be ripped on for months.'

Axel grins slightly, amused. He quickly refocuses his thoughts and places a hand on Delilah's shoulder, again serious.

'Just don't go rubbing salt in that wound, okay? Try and keep that fire in check for me, please.'

'I will, Dad.'

'Promise?'

'Promise.'

The sound of a gunshot jolted Delilah from her thoughts. She flinched slightly. She instantly knew it was in her head, but sometimes it would come from nowhere in dreams, daydreams, or more often in nightmares. Five years on from the bank job that ended it all, and the gunshot never lost its clarity.

Behind Delilah, the crumpled bedsheets rustled. A handsome young Latino man pulled himself out from under them with a groan, knocking an empty bottle of tequila off the nearby nightstand as he went. Completely naked, he took a few steps and retrieved his pants from the floor and pulled them on. Delilah ignored him.

'I gotta take a leak,' he said, rubbing his eyes as he headed towards the bathroom door at the far end of the room. Delilah glanced over to him.

'No,' she said flatly.

The guy raised an eyebrow, perplexed.

'What's the problem? I'll just be a second,' he said irritably.

Delilah took a drag on her cigarette and looked away from him.

'I said no, or are you as deaf as you are quick in bed?'

She blew out a long stream of smoke. The guy scoffed incredulously.

'Fuck you then, bitch.'

'You just did. You can go now,' replied Delilah nonchalantly as she flicked more ash onto the floor.

After taking a moment to register that she was, in fact, serious, the guy shook his head, picked up his shirt and shoes, and exited the room with a deliberate slam of the door. Delilah extinguished her cigarette in a nearby coffee cup, stood, and stretched. The young guy had been a brief distraction, picked up from the bar across the road from the motel to service her needs, nothing more. Delilah couldn't remember the last time she had made love as opposed to just having sex. Thinking about it sometimes made her sad, but there was often an easy solution for that. She reached over to the half-full tequila bottle resting on the adjacent side table and took a hearty swig. Together with the cigarette, that was breakfast taken care of.

Bottle in hand, she walked over to the bathroom, opened the door, and stepped into the windowless room's darkness. She flicked on the fluorescent lights. A rickety extractor fan kicked into life. The figure in the bathtub stirred. Ernesto Guzman's hands were tied to the taps, his mouth was taped over, and headphones covered his ears. Even though he was blindfolded, he seemed to register the presence of another person in the room. He started to groan through the duct tape, but Delilah ignored him.

She headed over to the sink, set the tequila bottle down, and took a moment to stare at herself in the mirror. She had not removed her mascara from the previous evening. It had started to run down her cheeks, the moisture from aggressive, sweaty sex acting as a substitute for tears. The lining around her eyes only highlighted how half-dead they looked. Delilah had dipped a toe into the waters of drug abuse a few years back but had retreated before it was too late. She knew she would have drowned and so could at least claim the small victory of looking relatively normal rather than some emaciated junkie wastrel. Instead, Delilah had opted for the marginally less self-destructive pursuits of part-time alcoholism, promiscuous sex, and, when nothing else would satisfy her, bare-knuckle cage fighting in a few biker drinking pits she frequented. She often won, and the money could be good, but she did it as much to help her feel something, even pain. It was becoming increasingly difficult to feel anything.

The biker haunts were also good sources of information for potential jobs. When Delilah had first arrived in Texas, keen to put as many miles as she could between herself and New York, she had attempted to find a use for her skills and training, but the heist scene was poorly developed. Any joker with a ski mask and a water pistol thought he was a modern-day John Dillinger. Instead, she had found more lucrative work as hired muscle for various shady elements. Their initial skepticism had quickly dissipated when exposed to her supreme marksmanship and unarmed combat proficiency against opposition twice her size. Her descent into ignominy, already well underway after New York, was accelerated. The past five years had been a blur of various dirty and often violent jobs, any of them acceptable for the right fee, which she would invariably waste on self-indulgence until it was time to work again.

The young Mexican writhing in the dry bathtub was just such a job. Delilah wasn't stupid. She didn't know anything about him before she was provided with a photograph and name. Still, it was clear that he was a narco, a member of Mexico's numerous competing drug cartels. She was also savvy enough to realize that her potential employers, represented by two shadowy and unsmiling Mexicans sitting in a shady bar, were also narcos, no doubt rivals to Guzman's cartel. Turning the job offer down hadn't been an option. She would likely have ended up in pieces in the desert. So she had accepted, promising to somehow get to Guzman during his upcoming party week in Las Vegas and deliver him into her employers' custody. She didn't want to think about what would happen to him after that. It wasn't her problem as long as the money was good.

The job had at least allowed her to exercise some of her skills in reconnaissance and surveillance, this time focused on an individual instead of a physical place. It revealed that Guzman had a favorite strip club he frequented every night after his copious drinking and gambling sessions. Maybe because he was in the United States instead of some violent Mexican border city, Guzman was only ever accompanied by two bodyguards instead of an entire entourage. The night before last, Delilah had spent hours beautifying herself, choosing the right heels to complement her legs and the best dress to make the most of her cleavage. She had deliberately set out to look like a porn star and had used her overt sexuality and inherent air of danger to quickly catch Guzman's eye.

Her seduction efforts - aided in no small part by the drug she had slipped into his drink - paid off. She had led him into the private booths at the rear of the club for a personal dance, the management having been paid to look the other way. By the time she had stripped to her lingerie, the drug had rendered Guzman unconscious. Five minutes later and he was in the back of a nondescript van, thrown in by a pair of burly bikers Delilah often had dealings with, the two bodyguards out cold in a nearby dumpster after receiving batons to the back of their heads. An hour later and Guzman was tied up in the bathtub he currently resided in, and all Delilah could do was wait for her employers to show up. She had spent the next day resting and then visited the bar across the road looking for a distraction, which had been duly found in the young barfly's company. An early morning text message had woken her an hour previously. They were coming.

Delilah finished considering the sad figure that gazed back at her from the mirror, grabbed a nearby towel, dampened it, and scrubbed the makeup from her face. She picked up a nearby water bottle, moved over to Guzman, and indelicately ripped the duct tape from his mouth.

'Ah, you bitch!' he yelled in heavily accented but clear English.

Delilah removed his headphones. Tinny rock music could be heard on loop.

'Morning sunshine,' she replied. 'Baby want his bottle?'

'Fuck you, you're dead!'

'Well, I think we'd better wash out that potty mouth, don't you?'

She unscrewed the bottle open and poured the contents over Guzman's face, causing him to cough and splutter. He shook away the excess water and started laughing.

'Wanna let me in on the joke?' quizzed Delilah.

'It's just funny to me how dead you are, and you don't even know it,' replied Guzman between chuckles. 'Sure, you're walking around now, but my brother Pablo, he'll find you and-'

'By the time he's done with me, I'll be begging for death, right? Somethin' like that?'

'Yeah, only he won't grant your wish. He'll keep it going for days, weeks even. I've seen it. He has a personal collection of videos. I'll start my own one with you.'

Delilah tutted and ripped off a stretch of duct tape from a roll left near the taps.

'So much good TV these days, and you still choose to watch shit like that.'

She leaned over, the tape ready to place over his mouth.

'But that's nothing compared to what he'll do to your family,' said Guzman spitefully.

Delilah paused a moment, considering what had been said.

'I don't have a family,' she said flatly.

She leaned in and stuck the tape over his mouth and replaced the headphones over his ears. She walked out of the bathroom, switching the light off as she went and closed the door behind her.

Delilah quickly scooped her loose belongings into a small backpack, pulled on some dusty boots, dark jeans, and a black leather jacket. There was a sharp knock at the main door. She opened it to find the same two burly Mexicans who had offered her the job. She nodded her head towards the bathroom. Nothing needed to be said. One of the Mexicans considered her carefully for a moment before throwing a thick brown envelope at her. Delilah didn't open it to count the money inside. She just wanted to get away and buried her unease as best she could.

The Mexicans parted ways. Delilah stepped through them, her head bowed slightly as she headed towards her car. It was a Gran Torino, which she had painted a shiny scarlet, probably the only possession that she put any time and love into. She started it up with a roar and swung it onto the road with a rooster tail of dust from the dirt parking area. Delilah had no idea where she was going, nor did she care.

3

Bethany sipped the hot, sweet tea, gently returned the delicate cup back to its saucer, and placed them down on the circular table before her. It was covered by a smooth, pearly white cloth. At its center was a small tower of three platters, each carrying a range of triangular sandwiches and cakes of different shapes and colors. Afternoon tea at the country club had quickly become a mid-week tradition after one of the wives had introduced it following her family's return from living in London. Bethany enjoyed it because it reminded her of that city and the freedom she had experienced during her own time there. Everything else about the occasion frustrated her, but she kept such thoughts hidden behind a pleasant and semi-permanent smile. She had faked almost everything about herself for the past five years, so concealing her disdain for most of the company that surrounded her presented little challenge.

As soon as she had separated from her sisters, Bethany had traveled to John F. Kennedy International Airport. She had boarded a flight as Bethany Andrews, a typical young backpacker determined to travel after graduating college. Much to her regret, Bethany had never actually been, but her alter ego was a graduate in art history, or so she claimed to anyone who asked. She was sufficiently well-read to carry through the act convincingly. It became a minor thrill to interact with new people as she made her way from Rome to Paris to Amsterdam to London, taking her blank page of a life and continuously sketching out new and varied backstory details as the whim took her.

The more time elapsed, the more Bethany began to feel that the new person she was becoming was more faithful to who she really was, or was always meant to be. She was intelligent, curious, academic, and cultured. The Bethany of old - the one who could shoot well, who could drive any vehicle with the best of them, the girl who could adopt a variety of personas to help scout out or infiltrate scores - was fading away like the details of a dream, increasingly difficult to remember before being lost entirely.

Bethany had arrived in London and decided to stay. Despite the transfers of funds provided by Jimmy, she had been overzealous in her spending and had enjoyed becoming the new Bethany a little too much. She had managed to secure a job as a barista in an upscale hipster cafe and found a house to share with some drama and art students, where she reveled in the discussions, parties and cultural activities they took part in. There were no plans for the future. She had simply enjoyed living in the present, not having to worry about the law kicking down the door or memorizing the next score's intricacies. At times, Bethany found herself missing the adrenaline rush of those days, but she pushed such thoughts out of her mind, closing her ears to their seductive whispers. She was no longer that person. Life was good, safe, predictable. Boring.

Six months into that new life, an unexpected but not unwelcome element had come along to upset it. His name was David. He was tall, fair-haired, handsome, a little older, and had walked into her cafe one quiet, sunny afternoon dressed in a simple sweater and jeans, a book tucked under his arm. He had smiled warmly, ordered an espresso, pulled out some reading glasses, and sat quietly studying the book. A curious Bethany had glanced at the cover. Her heart had leaped at seeing it involved art history. As the only person on shift and with no one else to serve, she had started engaging David in small talk about the book and her own, fictitious college studies and genuine travels through European museums. His New England accent had reminded her of America, of home.

The small talk had turned into an entire afternoon's discussion, which in turn had given way to evening drinks. The chemistry between them had been instantaneous and warmly welcome. David worked in finance and was on a year's transfer in London, but he was clear that it was not his life, that he enjoyed what he did but valued some things more than money. They had started dating. After three months, she had moved into his modest apartment. They had lived simply but happily. Bethany had continued to live in the moment, not thinking about what the future held. Then the choice came.

David had been recalled to his company in New York. He wanted her to come with him. He knew he loved her and wanted to marry her, but there was something she needed to know first. He had not considered it necessary to mention before because it had no impact on who he was as a person, on his hopes, dreams, and, above all, loves. But, when he had said he had been recalled to his company, he had meant exactly that; *his* company. David Friedman of Friedman Associates, one of the largest hedge funds in the United States, a company and family with over a century of pedigree on Wall Street to which he was the heir. David's time in London had allowed him to escape what could be a suffocating environment, one he was reluctantly compelled to return to. It would be made infinitely more bearable if Bethany were there by his side.

Still, she had to know what exactly she would be joining, what kind of life it would involve leading. She would want for nothing and, most importantly, would be loved for who she was. But David had been equally clear that such a life's privileges also had a cost, principally the often invisible but no-less-present bars of a gilded cage made up of social expectations and class prejudice.

Bethany had thought carefully about what he had said. It had been difficult to process that she would have gone from robbing people like David to being on the verge of joining his social set in just under a year. It was like a fairytale, a dashing prince sweeping a poor girl off to the palace to become his princess. Could she return to New York, knowing her old life was so close, just a short subway ride away, but forever out of reach? Even if, by some miracle, Jimmy ever contacted her on the burner phone she kept hidden, it would be impossible to return to being Bethany Archer if she chose to fully embrace her new life, rather than treat it as if it were a sabbatical. It was Bethany Andrews with whom David had fallen in love. She had had to decide which Bethany would live and which would die.

***

There were times when Bethany Friedman wondered if she had indeed made the right choice, and the afternoon tea sessions were just such occasions. Surrounded by fellow wives and girlfriends of Manhattan's elite, she was all too aware of the invisible bars that David had spoken of. Was she wearing the right dress? Was she saying the right things? Did a particular look from one of the wives mean that Bethany had accidentally slipped into her old Brooklyn accent despite her best efforts to soften and change it? Had she committed one of a myriad of potential other social sins?

The Queen Bee of the group was undoubtedly
Kristin Hamilton, who sat directly opposite Bethany,
occasionally glancing at her with suspicion, as if she
could sense the social imposter who had somehow
managed to infiltrate the exclusive country club on Long
Island. Flowing blonde curls, flawless skin, designer
dress, and a diamond bracelet that doubtless could have
bought the house Bethany grew up in; all were clear
signs of Kristin's wealth, status and privilege, prominent
even before her marriage to a fellow blue-blood. She
exuded the manner of someone who would have
considered even the Hamptons to be low-rent. Bethany
had taken an instant dislike to the woman when they had
first met. Still, she had persevered because David and
Kristin's husband, Chad, were part of the same set.

David found them equally obnoxious but had
become desensitized to it after years of growing up
surrounded by such people, not least his parents, who
had not been exactly overjoyed to see him return to New
York with a new and already-pregnant wife in tow whom

they had never met, much less had a chance to approve of. They had eventually accepted her, if not warmed to the reality, a situation that best described the ladies Bethany sat with. She sensed that she had been invited to the afternoon teas and other getaways out of social obligation rather than a desire for her company. Bethany played the game anyway, placated by David's love and their mutual devotion to Lily.

Little Lily Friedman, three and a half years old. Next to her marriage, it was the main thing that gave Bethany's life meaning and purpose. The little girl had been named in honor of Bethany's mother, Lilian Archer, to keep some part of her true heritage alive. Everything had changed the day Lily had been born. Whenever Bethany felt like unleashing a primal scream, all she had to do was think of her daughter, and any anger and frustration melted away. She insisted on raising the child herself rather than passing her off to a full-time nanny like many of the wives had done. It was their prerogative, Bethany tried not to judge, but none of them were working mothers. It just seemed a convenient way of ensuring their blue-bloodlines continued while they shopped, vacationed, and practiced yoga unburdened by nighttime crying and dirty diapers. Bethany's thoughts had drifted towards Lily's nursery activities when she caught herself and sought to reengage in the conversation unfolding before her. Of course, conversation implied two-way traffic, but Kristin was firmly set on transmit and the others to receive.

'So then we flew to Rome at the last minute, all for the sake of a painting Chad absolutely had to have,' explained Kristin casually, as if it were just a trip across town. 'I can't tell you how hot it was there. Thank God his uncle owns a villa in the country. I could cool off by the pool while he went antique shopping. That boy does love his collection.'

'But Kristin darling, I thought you loved Rome?' queried one of her acolytes named Evangeline. 'Isn't that where you and Chad met?'

'No dear,' dismissed Kristin with a shake of her head. 'You're thinking of Paris.'

'Well, if you're going to meet your future love, then I guess Paris is the best place for it,' ventured Bethany as she decided to try and contribute. 'You know, city of romance.'

Kristin considered her with a slight smile. She did a poor job of disguising either pity or contempt, Bethany couldn't tell which.

'Call me old fashioned, but I think love can blossom anywhere, regardless of place.'

Everyone glanced towards the lady who had opined the sentiment. Senator Catherine Dent was one of the few that Bethany not only had time for but actively respected and admired. Tall and elegant, with dark grey hair, only slightly faded beauty and a seductively husky voice, Catherine would have had every right to declare herself the most blue-blooded of them all. She was the matriarch of one of New York's oldest and most respected families, the widow of a United States senator appointed to his seat on merit after his death, who then backed it up with an election victory of her own. Once the head of her own successful venture capital firm, which quietly ticked away while she crafted a name in the Senate, Catherine carried herself with humility and grace. It was what had caused Bethany to be instantly drawn to her when they had first met at a party a few months prior.

While not a regular at the afternoon tea parties, on occasions during recess Catherine would find herself at the club following lunch or a spa session and would be eagerly invited over by the wives if they spotted her. Whether at receptions, dinner parties, or other social gatherings, it was clear that all of the ladies around the table, Kristin included, were in awe of the venerable lady. When she spoke, they listened.

'Take David and Bethany here,' continued Catherine. 'You met in London, right? Historic, yes. Wet, certainly. Romantic? Well, perhaps in Hollywood's eyes anyway.'

She smiled as the rest of the ladies gigged obligingly. 'Personally, I love a Cinderella story.'

She winked supportively at Bethany while Kristin tilted her head a little.

'Yes, that's right, you were a waitress in a cafe, weren't you?' she probed, though she knew full well Bethany's story since David had unashamedly not shied away from telling it. Whereas Catherine had found it a delightful tale and had told Bethany as much in private, it was clear that Kristin saw it as a button to push.

'That's right,' acknowledged Bethany neutrally. She took another sip of tea, resisting the urge to throw it in Kristin's face. 'And a barista too if you want to get technical.'

'Is that so?' remarked Kristin with feigned interest. She placed a hand under her chin and considered Bethany as she would a fascinating exhibit. 'Maybe I'll come visit for a coffee sometime, help you relive the glory days.'

Bethany considered her a moment before slowly nodding with a smile.

'That would be lovely.'

***

Bethany repeatedly slammed the steering wheel of her Mercedes with her fists, screaming as she did so. She caught herself and stopped, breathless. Sheepishly, she looked around but thankfully saw no witnesses to her tantrum. She brushed some loose hair back behind her ear, and calmly started the car. It took a moment to navigate towards the exit road of the vast country club. She passed rows of sports cars and SUVs as she did, occasionally stopping to let groundskeepers cross in front of her. She stopped at the mouth of the exit road, a long trail that snaked its way downhill through half a dozen hairpin turns. If Bethany had been the girl she once was, she would have thought nothing of flooring the accelerator and executing tight drifts on each turn, the rear tires smoking and screaming in distress.

Screw it.

Bethany leaned down, opened the glove compartment, and extracted her leather driving gloves and a pair of sleek shades. The latter went on first, then she slowly pulled on both gloves, flexing her fingers, feeling the stretch of the leather. She gripped the steering wheel hard, checked her rear-view mirror to find it empty, and eased her foot up and down on the accelerator. Instinctively, Bethany had always known why she had opted to buy a rear-wheel drive, manual version of her Mercedes when everyone else she knew drove automatics. She had resisted the call to act irresponsibly but knew she would concede to it eventually. Besides, almost everything in her life now was like an automatic, carefully shifting up and down as the pace required, all too predictably, all too unexceptionally, out of her hands. But not this. Over this, she had complete control. The engine purred, the powerful revs seemingly flowing from the front, through her legs, up her spine and charging her brain. She let the desire, anticipation, and borderline lust build up until she could contain them no longer. They demanded release.

She dropped the handbrake and floored the accelerator. The Mercedes took off at pace, forcing her back into her seat. She quickly gathered speed as she switched gears and within seconds had hit sixty on the speedometer, seventy, eighty. The spaces either side of the road became a blur. All there was in the world, all that mattered, all that was sharp and in focus, was the road itself and the upcoming hairpin, a full one-eighty degree turn. Bethany slammed the brakes and clutch and turned the wheel hard to the left. She dropped down several gears by skipping from high to low and floored the accelerator again. The car's rear snapped out, but she maintained control, the tires screeching and smoking just as she had anticipated, the sound and smell causing her to break into giddy whoops. Bethany was master of the beast. It could buck all it liked, but she owned it.

Bethany flicked the rear back into place, and the car straightened up again. Instantly she continued up the gears, repeating the same sequence until she hit another bend, then another. There were a few more turns to conquer, but she reluctantly eased off and slowed her speed to the usual sensible level. It would have been too risky to have continued. She was surprised not to have encountered anyone on the way down and thanked her luck for not having to explain herself and risk expulsion from the club. Too many questions would have flowed from that. What was she thinking? What would people say? And most concerning, where did she learn to drive like that?

By the time Bethany reached the club's gated entrance at the end of the road, her car had appeared to have taken a straightforward, uneventful, and leisurely trip down from the main complex. Inside, her heart raced like a jackhammer. The adrenaline rush had barely faded, but she feigned calm. Bethany waved at the guard like she always did when he let her through. He, in turn, waved her off like he always did as she turned right. To him, to the ladies, to the world, even to the man she loved, the sweet, quiet, and perfectly ordinary Bethany Friedman was headed home. But for a brief moment, Bethany Archer had been back in control. And for the briefest of moments, she had wanted to turn left.

4

The crunch of bodies never failed to make Angie wince, even when she stood on the sidelines, a fair distance away. The Harrington Academy football team was having a good game, which made her and her fellow cheerleaders' job all the easier. School spirit was already riding the crest of a high wave. All they had to do was help shepherd it along and make sure it didn't peter out until the final whistle was blown. A time out was called, and both teams huddled together with their coaches to discuss how to hammer home victory or lessen the margin of defeat. That was her cue.

As captain of the cheerleaders, Angie, leading her squad, bounded out in front of the home audience stands, her smile beaming. Five years had seen her face become more angular, her chin and cheekbones more defined, her blue eyes still just as piercing. It would have been a dream find for a modeling agency talent spotter in another life. She possessed a taller, leaner physique, every muscle and sinew sculpted by endless hours spent at ballet classes and subsequent gymnastics training when her interest in the former waned. She and her squad were dressed in yellow and black Lycra outfits, reflecting the colors of the football team, the Harrington Hornets. It was shirts and pants for the guys, vests and mini-skirts for the girls. Angie, similarly-colored ribbons in her blonde pigtails, gentle makeup highlighting her eyes and cheekbones, took her place at the head of the squad, and they began their choreographed routine.

It was no challenge for Angie, one of the quick and easy options in their repertoire, rehearsed mentally and physically a hundred times, so ingrained that she could afford to detach herself from what was going on. Half of the time, the challenge was not to look bored. She still enjoyed the more challenging displays, whether executing multiple backflips or being tossed high into the air, pirouetting as much as she could before gravity took hold and she landed back in the arms of her squad. Of course, those were nothing compared to the efforts she put into her gymnastics, where she would spend hours practicing on the pommel horse, still rings and parallel bars.

People often questioned Angie on how she found the time to fit in all her extracurricular activities and achieve one of the highest grade point averages at the school. In reality, it was easy when she had nowhere to go during weekends and holidays, her fictitious parents constantly jet-setting. Angie always just shrugged and simply said she made the time. It made her sound disciplined, well-planned, and committed. She was indeed all three but had had little choice in order to make her cover work for her so that the world - or more accurately the bubble she inhabited - believed without question in whom she appeared to be. Angie Archer had been a rebellious, tomboyish, plain-spoken Brooklynite teen, often glued to her laptop while she took the first tentative steps into the world of hacking. Angelina Fairchild was a conforming, feminine, well-spoken young woman on the cusp of attending any Ivy League college she wished. Many would have been envious of her position, but she could not celebrate what she had never asked for. As the squad finished their routine, Angie held her arms up to rapturous applause from the home crowd and flashed her brilliant smile, just one of the many lies she had learned to hide behind.

***

'Oh my God, Ange, did you see how Greg looked at you tonight?' queried Faye, a member of Angie's cheerleader squad, as she dried her hair. 'He wants you, bad.'

'Maybe for my ass, definitely not for my brain,' scoffed Angie as she tied her own hair into a tight bun.

'And?' responded Faye, mystified as to why it would matter. 'Have you seen *his* ass?'

'No, but *you've* clearly been checking it out. Why don't you try your luck?'

'I would, but Mark and I are going steady now.'

'For all of five minutes,' noted Angie with a raised eyebrow. 'Or is it true love already?'

'Hell no, it's just fun. But we're all out of here next summer, so may as well enjoy the ride while we can.'

As Faye proceeded to recount her discrete sexual encounters with Mark, Angie let her thoughts drift. It was just another example of the typical asinine conversations that dominated the ladies' locker room, not just after games but on most occasions. If it wasn't about boys, it was about vacations to foreign lands, new cars, new clothes, and schoolwork pressures and stresses.

Try watching your sister bleeding all over the place or have your father rot in prison and then talk to me about stress, Angie would think.

But, as always, she would simply nod in agreement. She held no resentment for the other girls' petty concerns. She liked most of them. But she had no real friends as such, more like people she was friendly with. To possess a true friend was to have someone you could confide in, rely on, and talk with in-depth about your life. But for five years, the only person Angie felt she could rely on had been herself, despite Jimmy's best efforts at sending anonymous care packages or attempts at semi-regular meetings. After a while, she had started making up excuses for why she couldn't meet as often and then not meet at all. Not because she didn't want to see him, but because he was too painful a reminder of her past.

That was also the problem with getting close to people. Angie's past life was off-limits. Her new one was entirely superficial, from the photoshopped images of her and her 'parents' together, to the refined accent she had worked hard to adopt in those first few weeks but now had become natural to her. She had joined the drama society as soon as she could, not for fun but for research, to help perfect the accent and craft a new persona. She had been the ultimate method actor for five years now, but that was the fundamental problem when it came to getting close to someone. How could she ever be completely open and honest with a friend or even a lover when almost every word she spoke was a lie?

'You coming to the party?' asked Faye, dragging Angie's mind back from its wandering.

'You know me, I wouldn't miss it,' lied Angie, knowing exactly where she preferred to be, and it wasn't the festivities at the senior student's common room. 'I've got to call my parents first, though, so I'll be a little late,' she continued.

'Sure, no problem,' said Faye as she pulled her jacket on and readied to leave. 'Don't be too late, or Greg may have taken himself off the market.'

Angie rolled her eyes, smiled, and waved Faye off. Once she was sure she was alone, she threw her cheerleading uniform into her locker. She pulled out a small backpack that held what she regarded as her true uniform. Angie opened it up and raised a genuine smile.

Angie stuck to the shadows of the main school building, the old part that still carried the Nineteenth Century grandiosity of plush red carpets and polished dark wood-paneled walls. Ornate paintings were spaced out with marked precision. Every so often, a piece of furniture, a sculpture, or even a suit of armor standing guard like a sentinel was placed between the oil landscapes and portraits of past faculty members. It was dark outside, and the lights of the corridors were so dim as to be non-existent. It made it easy for Angie to stealthily make her way, with her pants, turtleneck sweater, ski mask, and small utility belt, all of them jet-black in color, effectively camouflaging her.

Angie paused a few feet away from the mouth of a third-floor corridor that led to the senior faculty members' offices. She knew a security camera was pointed down the corridor towards her direction of approach, but that it aimed down from a high angle and could not see the ceiling. Angie looked up and found the thick wooden support beam she was counting on. It ran along the length of the corridor she presently found herself standing in, but was connected to another beam which shot off at a right angle down the ceiling of the corridor protected by the camera.

She opened one of her utility belt pouches and produced a pair of thin gloves with grippy rubber palms and fingertips. She pulled them on, crouched down low, breathed deeply several times and jumped upwards with explosive force, finding small grooves either side of the beam to dig her fingers into. Simultaneously she used the momentum to latch her knees and sneaker soles onto the beam. Angie started pulling herself along as quickly as she could, conscious that the muscle pressure she was applying to fix her grip was only as strong as the energy she had available, which was finite. She would stretch her arms out first, locate grip, then pull her legs towards her torso, squeezing the beam with her calves and knees to maintain position and control as she progressed. It reminded her of an upside-down caterpillar crawl, but Angie doubted a caterpillar's muscles burnt from lactic acid as rapidly as hers were.

She quickly reached the off-shoot beam that followed the corridor towards the senior faculty area and delicately transferred herself to it. She continued the same maneuver until she had cleared the security camera. She loosened her leg muscles and let them dangle. She hung on momentarily before she silently dropped to the ground and checked both directions. So far, so good.

The corridor in which she found herself was where the administrators for each academic department had their offices. At the end of it lay another one, nicknamed the 'Corridor of Power' by the students, for to turn right was to find the offices of the Dean of Faculty and Dean of Students and to turn left was to visit the office of the Dean of Academic Affairs and, for those really in trouble, the Headmaster's office. Angie quietly made her way leftwards and stopped at the door belonging to the Dean of Academic Affairs. She tried the handle but found it locked, as expected.

She knelt down and produced a lock pick from her utility belt and set to work on the simple lock just beneath the handle. It only took a few seconds before she heard a gentle click and slowly rotated the lock. Another click followed a second later, but it was louder and came from her left. Angie turned in horror to find the Headmaster's personal assistant emerge from his office, carrying a small collection of files. It was only twenty feet or so down the corridor, and all the PA had to do was turn right and she would see Angie brazenly attempting an act of breaking and entering. The PA would doubtless scream, run, raise the alarm, call the police, and the situation would spiral ever downwards. Angie silently cursed herself for not checking the environment was entirely clear. It had been one of her father's cardinal lessons in his tradecraft, imparted to her sisters during their early education down in the family basement, which Angie had snuck into to discreetly observe when everyone thought she was in bed.

The PA turned to her left and fiddled in her handbag for her keys. Angie knelt frozen, daring not to breathe. As the PA found the keys, she had leaned to the side too much and several of the files from the top of the pile slid off and spilled their contents on the floor. The PA tutted, knelt down, placed the intact files to the side, and started collecting the scattered paperwork. The distraction represented Angle's only chance, and she knew it. Opening the Dean's door would have been too loud. She needed another escape. Angie stuck the lock pick between her teeth, checked both directions, and up at the ceiling. There was no wooden support beam on this stretch to latch on to. The only salvation she could see was a sturdy side table with a silver horse sculpture resting upon it.

She dashed for it, grateful that the plush carpet helped disguise her footfalls, but she knew it would not be enough. The darkness of the corridor, mitigated only by the moonlight which shone through the windows, would make any person feel slightly on edge and thus their perception more acute. It was human nature, and the PA was no different. She paused from collecting the papers, convinced she had heard something but could not place its source. She most definitely then heard a dull thud and spun around, her heart racing, but only saw a clear corridor. She shivered slightly and shrugged it off. In her years working at Harrington, she had heard all manner of sounds that gave credence to some of the ghost stories that surrounded the place. Yet for each one, the maintenance staff had assured or even shown her that the cause was related to aging pipework, electrics, or crumbling masonry, rather than the supernatural. She finished gathering the paperwork into the proper files, picked them up with a tighter grip, and locked the Headmaster's office.

Angie watched the PA walk down the corridor towards her position. She had braced herself up high, her legs and arms outstretched, forcing themselves against both walls. For all intents and purposes, she had turned herself into a human plank, facing downwards. She had used the side table as a launch to run-up to and pounce off to get herself in position, her speed just enough to get into place before the spooked PA clocked her, even with the dull thud it had caused. But it was only a temporary solution. Angie's stomach muscles were already starting to protest. Soon they would begin to scream, as would her arms and legs. It would be fine though, she could maintain it for a little while longer, just enough for the PA to cross under her and continue on to-

The PA stopped directly beneath Angie as her phone pinged inside her handbag. Clutching the files close to her chest, she reached in with her free hand and produced the phone, opening it to read a long text message that had been sent. As the PA giggled at what appeared to be a joke, Angie closed her eyes. She tried to focus her mind anywhere else other than on the immediate burning sensation spreading across her torso and limbs.

The ski mask soaked up the sweat that would have otherwise started dripping right on top of the PA. Angie opened her eyes and unleashed an internal scream when she saw the PA texting back whichever asshole comedian had chosen that exact moment to send a funny. Her arms and legs had started shaking and were close to failing. Mental determination had nothing to do with it. The body was only capable of so much physical endurance before crying for a time out.

Finally, the PA sent her reply and continued walking, rounding the corner into the corridor with the security camera and disappearing from sight. Angie gave it a few seconds to be sure then released herself, dropping down and lowering into an immediate crouch to absorb the fall. She fought the urge to curl up into a whimpering fetal position and quickly entered the office of the Dean of Academic Affairs, locking it behind her.

Secure in the knowledge that she was safe in the darkened room, Angie pulled the lock pick from her teeth and let out a gasp. She leaned forwards against the wall, stretching her limbs to wash away the lactic acid and ward off cramp. After a couple of minutes, she felt better and turned her attention to her primary goal. The office was dominated by bookshelves. In the center was a large ornate wooden desk upon which rested the Dean's office phone and computer. Angie headed for the computer and pulled out a thumb drive from her utility belt. The terminal was asleep, so she tapped the keyboard to wake it and, as predicted, was confronted with a password request screen. It didn't matter.

She located a USB port and inserted the thumb drive. The hours she had spent building the necessary malware paid off. Within a minute, she had not only gained access to the system but downloaded every file she sought onto the thumb drive. Harrington's academic ethos may have been venerable, but their cybersecurity policy certainly wasn't. With opportunities so rare, it presented Angie with a perfect chance to put the cheerleader persona in a box where it belonged and let her true self come out to play.

She pocketed the thumb drive and restored the computer to its previous state. Not the tech-savviest of people, the Dean would doubtless detect nothing out of the ordinary when he returned to his desk on Monday morning. Angie considered her options and decided against returning the way she had come. She had scouted the exterior of the Dean's office earlier in the week and knew that a drain pipe ran past one of the windows, concealed amidst a batch of thick ivy that clung to the outside wall.

She opened the nearby window, crawled out, made sure she had a good foothold on the pipe and a firm grip with her right hand. She used her left to pull the window closed with a click and slowly made her way down. After a minute, she hopped off onto the soft grass, whipped her ski mask off, closed her eyes, and breathed deeply, enjoying the cool evening air on her face.

'Feels good, doesn't it, the high?'

A startled Angie spun around, her heart missing a beat. She found Jimmy standing a few feet away, slightly grayer and slightly fatter, but otherwise little different from the last time she had seen him the previous Christmas holidays, almost ten months prior. Angie had finally run out of excuses to avoid meeting him. She had taken the train to Manhattan and then the subway to the Brooklyn Museum, where they had spent the afternoon wandering the galleries, talking to each other without saying very much at all. Even back then, Angie had the impression that Jimmy suspected her extracurricular activities were not merely limited to cheerleading, gymnastics, and drama, but now those suspicions were confirmed. She chastised herself for the second time that evening for being sloppy in making sure her immediate environment was clear, the first time out of excitement, the second out of fatigue. Both were unacceptable.

'Jesus, you scared the shit out of me, Jimmy!' she reproached him, even though she knew full well that she was the one in error. 'Are you stalking me, or something?'

'I came to see how you were doing. It's not like you're calling every five minutes these days,' he replied flatly, his body still, hands buried in his jacket pockets. 'I waited for you to come out of the gym, then saw you sneak away, dressed like you were ready to break into the goddamn CIA.'

'So you followed me here? How'd you know I'd come down this way?'

'Cause I know you Angie Archer.'

'Don't call me that, that's not who I am anymore,' she said irritably.

'It might not be what you're *called* anymore, but it's sure as shit who you still *are*, whether you like it or not. The Angie I knew, the devil with a laptop, she couldn't resist breaking into the school system. There's just nothing else here that'd get your blood racing. One of the best places to do it, to give this little world the middle finger, is the senior faculty offices. You forgot that your dad and I scouted this place out for you before all the shit went down.'

'You got it all figured out, don't you?' said Angie with a bitter smile.

'Only because I follow the rules and one of the most important is never assume you're secure until you're back at base.'

'Yeah, I got that. I'll do better next time.'

'Does there have to be a next time?' asked Jimmy forlornly.

'I'm not having this conversation in the open,' replied Angie. 'In fact, I'm not having it at all.'

She turned and started in the direction of the girls' dormitories.

'Don't you walk away from me, young lady!' barked Jimmy.

'Keep your damn voice down!' hissed Angie.

'Don't worry. The kids are partying, and the staff are at a drinks reception. But you know that. That's why you chose this time to make your move.'

'Get your recon and timing right, and you're halfway there. Another one of Dad's rules, right?'

'Another one was don't take unnecessary risks for little gain,' said Jimmy as he tried to keep a lid on his swelling anger at her petulant attitude. 'What the hell are you doing, Angie? You could have been kicked out or even arrested, for what?'

'Exam questions for the next semester, if you must know.'

'Oh, so you're cheating now?'

Angie folded her arms and raised an eyebrow.

'So I should earn an honest grade, in the same way you earned an honest buck?'

'Touché,' Jimmy acknowledged humbly.

'You think I could get an offer from Harvard and hack most of the secure systems out there, and that I'd need to even think about casual cheating to get by?' she scoffed. 'These are for sale through my partner, just a little extra pocket money, that's all.'

Jimmy shook his head. He wasn't buying it.

'Bullshit, you get more than enough from the fund. You do it for the thrill, for the kicks, plain and simple, just like any other spoilt little rich girl.'

Angie's mouth dropped, aghast.

'Fuck you, Jimmy, you're not my father,' she retorted, wounded.

'I've been the closest you've had for five years,' he responded pridefully.

'Then maybe that's why I'd have been better off as an orphan.'

Angie had meant it to hurt. A part of her instantly regretted the words. But the part that embraced the spite, the part fueled by her pain, batted away the shame. She locked eyes with him for a moment then broke away. She turned and headed for the dorms, not looking back at a stunned Jimmy lest he saw the tears starting to form in her eyes. On the first day at Harrington, she had promised herself that no one would ever see her vulnerable again. Amidst a graveyard of dead commitments she had made to herself and others over the previous five years, that was one she intended to keep alive.

5

Jimmy gazed absentmindedly at the tumbler of scotch placed before him atop the bar. The ice that had come with it had long since melted. He glanced over to the football game showing on a nearby television screen. The New York Giants were struggling badly. If they kept playing like that for the next few games, they would have no chance of making a home Super Bowl at the Met Life Stadium in New Jersey. Jimmy may as well have rolled up the multiple hundred dollar bills he had spent securing a ticket and smoked them.

'You okay, Jimmy?' asked Lou, the aging bartender and owner of the establishment named after him. He dropped a couple of fresh ice cubes into the tumbler.

'I'm losing her, Lou,' said Jimmy with a sigh as he took a sip.

'Who? You got a girl now?'

'Nah, nothing like that, just... well, family, I guess.'

'Ah, the one thing guaranteed to put a smile on your face one minute and bring you to tears the next.'

Jimmy looked up at Lou and raised an eyebrow.

'That your only pearl of wisdom?'

'Nah, I got a drawer full of 'em in the back,' replied Lou with a grin.

'The barman is always prepared, right?' said Jimmy as he downed the remainder of the scotch.

'We're the fourth emergency service. You want another?'

Jimmy mulled the question a moment. He did want one, badly, but he rarely drank because he knew it wouldn't stop until either he was on the floor or Lou walked him home in the early hours. The prospect raised a little fear in him, but not because he was an alcoholic who risked relapse, far from it. For the past few years, Jimmy had tried to avoid confirming to the world what he felt inside; that he was a pathetic has-been with his best years in the rearview mirror and only barren lands on the road ahead. Pissing his life away up against a barroom wall would have gone some way to validating that fear.

Not that others didn't think it already. In the quiet of the late hours, the only patrons of Lou's Place were Jimmy and three young men. They congregated in one of the booths, a large collection of empty beer bottles assembled before them. They talked in whispered tones and occasionally glanced up at Jimmy and giggled to themselves. He had tried to ignore them as not worth his time, but his pride poked at him to do something about it. Yet it was best not to. The leader of the trio was Tony 'Two Toes' Giamatti, scion of the Giamatti crime family out of New Jersey. He was called Two Toes - though never to his face because it enraged him so - because he had accidentally shot off three others when playing around with a shotgun during a display of his supposed shooting prowess. What Tony and his lackeys were doing out in Brooklyn was a mystery, but its likely nefariousness was not.

Lou glanced over to them as they giggled. He frowned and shook his head.

'Young punks. They should have some more goddamn respect.'

'I used to be that cocky once,' conceded Jimmy.

'Behind closed doors maybe, never in a guy's presence,' protested Lou. 'I remember back when Gotti was on the scene, you didn't fuck with the Delgados.'

'Wrong,' countered Jimmy with a wag of his finger. 'You didn't fuck with my father or my brothers. Hell, they even made me shit my pants. It's half the reason I joined the army, to get out of here. And now I'm the only one left, end of the line.'

'The great survivor, huh?'

Jimmy sighed.

'I'm an old, blunt-toothed lion waiting for the younger cubs to make their move. The vultures are circling Lou, and I can't get out from under their shadow. Fuck it, I will have another.'

He tapped the empty tumbler, and Lou duly poured.

'I'll get that one gramps,' said Tony loudly from across the room. 'I ain't donated to charity for a while.'

The trio burst out laughing. Jimmy calmly sipped the scotch, but inside, something finally snapped. He turned on his stool and raised the glass.

'Here's to you, Two Toes.'

The laughing instantly stopped, and Tony's smile evaporated. He stood up, as did his two companions, and slowly started walking towards Jimmy.

'What did you say?' he demanded quietly but menacingly.

'You heard,' replied Jimmy, staring ahead and ignoring the approaching hothead.

'No, I don't think I did, you washed up old fuck.' Tony stopped next to Jimmy's left side, the two companions discreetly covering his right and rear. 'Could you repeat it?'

Jimmy turned to Tony, raised his glass, and finished the scotch.

'I said here's to you, you deformed little shit. Maybe you should have blown your dick off instead and done the gene pool a favor.'

Tony ran a knuckle over his teeth. He shook a little in barely restrained rage, breathed deeply, then grinned.

'You got a sharp tongue, Delgado. I think I'm gonna have to cut it out.'

As quickly as Tony had drawn his flick knife, Jimmy had grabbed the young man's wrist, pinned his face against the bar, taken the weapon for himself, and had the tip of the blade hovering over Tony's temple ready to drive downwards through his skull. The shocked companions drew their guns and aimed them at Jimmy.

'Let him fuckin' go!' cried one, his voice cracking with panic.

'Drop the guns, and you walk,' responded Jimmy as coolly as if ordering a pizza. 'Don't, and we'll see how much air is in this balloon.'

He tapped Tony's forehead with his free hand, further enraging the junior mobster.

'What are you waiting for? Kill this cocksucker!'

Everyone in the room turned when they heard the click of a pistol being taken off its safety. The bearer had managed to enter without anyone noticing and now aimed his weapon at Tony's companions.

Axel Archer cricked his neck.

'You both drop those pieces right now, or all three of you are dead in two-seconds, with time to spare.'

Jimmy's heart skipped a beat. For a moment, he forgot everything, even to breathe. He must have been dreaming, hallucinating maybe. Perhaps Tony and his goons had already stabbed or shot him, and he was having visions of what could have been as he bled out on the floor. But his long-time friend was really there, now fully-grey and bearded.

'Clock's ticking, assholes,' stated Axel forcefully. 'One, two-'

'Okay, okay!' yelled one of the companions, who placed his weapon on the floor, as did his partner a second later.

'Good, now get the hell out of here.'

Jimmy saw Axel nod at him and still took a moment to process that the whole scene was actually happening. He pulled Tony off the bar and shoved him into the arms of his goons, who started dragging him towards the exit despite his physical protestations.

'You're gonna regret this, Delgado, you hear me!' he screamed as he pointed threateningly at Jimmy. 'You're fuckin' dead, I promise you. No one disrespects me like that!'

'Don't forget to change his diaper,' Jimmy called out as the trio vanished through the door and into the night.

He turned his attention to Axel, who had pocketed his weapon.

'Tell me what's goin' on here, man, cause I can't think straight right now,' he pleaded.

Axel marched over and clasped his arms around Jimmy's muscular frame.

'It's so good to see you brother, you have no idea.'

Jimmy eased Axel away but kept supportive hands on his friend's shoulders.

'Axel, buddy, please, what's happening here? They release you early or somethin'? You're in for life last I heard. I mean, I wanted to come see you, please believe me, but you said we should never-'

Jimmy realized he was starting to speed up and babble when Axel shushed him.

'I get it, Jimmy, I do. You did everything right.' He sighed and swallowed hard. 'God, I got so much to tell you and not enough time.'

Jimmy instantly knew that something was very wrong. He had seen Axel try to hold back his emotions in such an obvious way only a handful of times during their friendship. The last occasion was when he had attempted to keep it together when telling the girls that Lilian, their mother, really was in her final hours without reprieve.

'There's just never enough time,' said Axel mournfully.

Jimmy squeezed his friend's shoulders.

'What are you talking about, brother? Tell me.'

'Do you remember the jetty near Dumbo, at the corner where Furman and Old Fulton streets meet?' asked Axel. 'We used to take the girls there for ice cream when they were little and watch the boats go by.'

'Yeah, I think so,' replied Jimmy, surprised at the question. He hadn't thought about the place in years.

'Meet me there in two hours. Don't be late. And bring protection.'

With that, Axel slapped Jimmy on the shoulder and quickly made for the exit.

'Wait, where are you goin'?' pleaded Jimmy, but Axel was gone and with him any hope of an immediate answer.

***

Jimmy shivered slightly in the chill night air. He gripped the pistol concealed in his jacket pocket. Bring protection, Axel had said, but for what and from whom?

It was late enough and cold enough that no one was around, and the nearby cafes and eateries had all closed. Maybe that was why Axel had chosen it as a meeting spot, but Jimmy doubted it. There were plenty of other places to ensure privacy and the area near Dumbo - short for Down Under the Manhattan Bridge Overpass - wasn't one of them. As soon as Axel had mentioned it, Jimmy could tell that it still retained sentimental value, and that seemed to be the primary reason it had been suggested. It was easy to see why.

The wooden jetty offered a commanding view of the Brooklyn Bridge as it crossed the East River's expanse. Across that body of water, the Manhattan skyline lit up the night. Even the jetty knew its privileged place, as, along the top of the railings that lined its perimeter, an artist had delicately carved the passages of a poem into the metal. Jimmy had no clue where they originated from, but the words '*Stand up tall masts of Manhattan, Stand up beautiful hills of Brooklyn*' stood out to him. He had finished rereading the words a third time when he heard footsteps from behind.

He turned to find Axel approaching him hurriedly.

'Thanks for coming,' he said.

'Jesus Christ, Axel, it wasn't like I was gonna hit the sack instead and catch you another time,' retorted Jimmy incredulously. 'Now, will you please quit dancin' and tell me what the fuck is goin' on?'

Axel looked at his watch and gazed out over the East River, the lights of the opposite bank shimmering on its inky black surface.

'I made a deal with the devil, Jim,' he said gloomily. 'I was looking at dyin' behind bars, never seein' my girls again, never sharin' a beer with you. I'd made my peace with that, not because I wanted to but because I had to, that if I didn't, I'd go nuts like half the lifers in the joint. Then two years ago, they came to me.'

'Who did?' probed Jimmy.

'It's best you don't know. Safest too. In any case, this explains it, or as much as I'm able anyway.'

Axel produced a plastic zip-lock bag from his jacket and handed it to Jimmy. It contained a micro SD card and a USB flash drive.

'The card has a video on it. When the time is right, play it to my girls. It'll tell you all you need to know and what to do with that drive.'

'But Axel, the girls are in the wind, like we planned. Except for Angie, she's okay.'

'I know she is. Bethany too.'

'But how could you-' began Jimmy before realization struck. Axel knew all about them, had been keeping track of them. 'How long have you been out?' he probed.

'Just long enough each time they needed me for a job. That was the deal. They'd get me out to plan their scores, lead their crew and get the job done before stickin' me back in until the next one. I'd buy my freedom permanently when they were finished with me. Either that or they'd suicide me, but it was worth the gamble. But I can't do it anymore, not with what they want me to get for them next.'

Axel's eyes teared up, and his voice started to break.

'Lilian knew that I was never truly a good man,' he continued. 'But I swore to her that I'd never be an evil man. And what they want to do, there's just no other word for it.'

'Then run! Disappear!' pleaded Jimmy.

'No can do, brother,' replied Axel, shaking his head.

He lifted his jacket to expose a scar on his torso.

'They got me on a leash. A tracking device buried deep, and I ain't no surgeon. But I skipped out on those fuckers a few hours ago, led them on a merry chase until I found you, and then led them by the nose again. But all chases got to end sooner or later. I just wish I could see my girls one last time. I guess this place and the memories are the best I'm gonna get. But then maybe that's the best I deserve.'

Axel and Jimmy turned as they heard the roar of an engine and the screech of tires from a vehicle just out of view. Axel turned back to Jimmy and raised a sharp salute.

'It's been my privilege serving with you James Delgado, never forget that.'

Jimmy was caught entirely by surprise as Axel grabbed his shoulders and shoved him over the jetty railing. He landed on the soft, wet sand a few meters below.

'What the hell!' he barked as he picked himself up.

'Hide yourself and whatever happens, stay quiet, or they'll kill you. You get that video to my girls, you swear to me.'

Before Jimmy could protest, Axel had stepped back and vanished from sight. Jimmy crawled up the natural rocky foundation of the jetty and crab-walked underneath the planks. He could barely see through the slits between each one but could generally hear what was going on above. Jimmy focused and made out what sounded like a vehicle slamming to a stop and multiple doors opening, followed by several sets of footsteps determinedly striding to the center of the jetty.

'Evening Butch,' he heard Axel say. 'Nice night for a walk, right?'

'Where's the package, Axel,' demanded a new voice, likely Butch.

'Nowhere you assholes are gonna find it,' replied Axel. 'I can't let you get your hands on that project. It's insanity.'

'It's for a cause bigger than you'll ever know!' raged Butch. 'You knew we weren't stealing Christmas lights, we never have been.'

'True, but this goes too far, and I want no part of it. This is the end for me, but if anythin' happens to my girls, to any of my friends, to the goddamn alley cat, then the *New York Times* and the Feds are goin' to get an interestin' delivery faster than you can say 'we're fucked', you understand me?'

'And you better understand that I can't let you go, Axel. We're gonna pull that package right out of your ass.'

'Give it your best shot.'

Jimmy heard the rustling of clothing, then a second later, a gunshot made him shudder. Half a second after that, three further shots boomed, followed by something heavy hitting the planks directly above him. He raised his face to a slit between planks and locked eyes with Axel. The latter's were open wide, darting around in their sockets. Jimmy heard pattering on the surface of his jacket. Blood was streaming through the slits. He bit his knuckle hard, desperate to scream out in rage, but he dared not.

'Son of a bitch!' yelled Butch. 'Fuck!'

Jimmy heard footfalls race to Axel, and he temporarily vanished from sight as the unseen assailants picked him up and frisked him. Distant police sirens began to wail, unmistakably getting louder with each passing second.

'Time to go, Butch!' said a new, unfamiliar voice.

'It ain't fuckin' here!' raged Butch. 'Come on, we're taking him with us.'

'I see the cops. We've got ten seconds, let's fuckin' go!' demanded the new voice.

They dropped Axel, and Jimmy heard them run. A few seconds later, a vehicle started and raced off. He rose and peered through the slit. Again he locked eyes with Axel, but this time his friend's orbs were still, empty. The light was extinguished.

'Oh Jesus,' Jimmy whimpered, trying and failing to control his emotions.

He indulged them for a brief moment, but then his training took over. He had a mission to complete, but more importantly, a promise to keep. His priority now was to get away and reevaluate what he was going to do. But, as Jimmy heard the police cars screech to a halt and the patrolmen rush out to secure the area, he couldn't do that from a jail cell. Nor was he prepared to risk camping out under the jetty all night, hoping that the police or forensics teams wouldn't discover him.

He felt for the ziplock bag in his jacket, confirmed it was there, and zipped up the pocket to be doubly safe. He quietly made his way to the waterline and waded out until he could swim. He doggy paddled over to an adjacent pier, ascended a ladder, avoided nearby lighting, and started jogging through the nearby Brooklyn Bridge Park, quickly losing himself in the numerous small walking paths and trees. He kept running until he reached the end of Furman Street, where it blended into Atlantic Avenue. He stopped, breathless.

Jimmy's thoughts raced as fast as his heart. For all the close calls he and Axel had had during their army years, they had always made it out, battered and bruised, but alive. Now Axel's luck had run out, and Jimmy could not fully comprehend the enormity of it. He pushed it to the back of his mind. He would deal with his loss later. During his service, he had made calls to the families of numerous dead comrades. It had never been easy. But

Jimmy knew the four calls he now needed to make would be the hardest of his life.

6

The large log fire burnt splendidly, casting a yellowish glow throughout the cabin's main area, aided by a few strategically placed oil lamps. Riley slept on a rug in front of the fireplace while Cole sat in a worn but comfortable leather armchair nearby. Cassidy approached wearing silk pajamas and a dressing gown, her hair loose and damp from the shower she had recently enjoyed. She carried two mugs and handed one to Cole before planting herself on a small couch opposite, also close to the fire.

'The Cassidy Special as requested, just the way momma used to make it,' she said and took a satisfying sip.

Cole took his own, and his eyes widened a little.

'I don't remember momma making cocoa with half a bottle of bourbon,' he said, trying to suppress a cough.

'Well, you have to entertain yourself any way you can out here,' she replied with a shrug and took another sip.

'Yeah, about that. What's with the whole 'living like the Unabomber' thing you got going on here? I ain't going to wake up to find my ass has been turned into a lampshade, am I?'

'Relax, I've had my share of liver and fava bean dinners for this month.'

'Glad to hear it, though, seriously Cass, you've dropped off everyone's radar. What's up? You quitting for real or you just on vacation?'

'More like going cold turkey for a while, see if it sticks,' she responded.

Cole raised a curious eyebrow.

'You say that like you're trying to kick some kind of addiction,' he ventured.

'Who's to say what we do isn't an addiction?' she asked as she stared into the fire.

'I don't follow.'

'Before I decided to come out here, it hit me that I'd been running and hiding for years. My sisters are doing God knows what now, but whatever it is, they made use of the second chance we had. Well, at least I'd like to think so. Me? I carried on exactly as before, just under a different name. Yeah, there was LA then Boston for a while, but even then, I never settled in one place for more than a few months. I can count the number of people I trust on one hand. Hell, I can't even remember the last time I woke up next to a warm body that wasn't the dog. For years, all I thought about was either the job I was on or the one that came after that, about landing bigger scores, to top the last thrill each time. I mean, Jesus, if that doesn't sound like addiction, then what the hell does?'

There was a moment's silence between them. The only sound was the crackling of the logs on the fire. Cole spoke first.

'You know, come to think of it, this is *exactly* the right amount of bourbon required for this conversation.'

He smiled, and Cassidy returned one, much to his delight.

'There you go girl, that's what I like to see.'

'I don't do it often.'

'Which means you should try it more.'

'But then I'd lose the mystique of the world thinking I'm a cold-hearted bitch.'

'This is true, but since your world right now is me and the dog, and I know you better, and he doesn't care, you've got no excuses.'

Cassidy chuckled and finished her cocoa.

'I've missed your bullshit,' she said.

'It *is* the finest,' Cole acknowledged as he finished his own mug.

'But you're still going to have to tell me why you're really here, sooner or later, you know that, right?'

Cassidy had not said it accusingly nor impatiently, just matter-of-factly. She knew there was more to Cole's reasoning for leaving Boston than simply feeling the authorities' heat, but she trusted him to tell her in his own time. That said, he needed to know that she knew, and with that understanding came responsibility on his part not to treat her like a fool. They had been through too much together for the trust and respect to start fraying.

'I will,' he said. 'Once I have it clear in my head, I will. I give you my word.'

'That's all I need to hear.'

More silence followed. After a few moments, Riley awoke and tilted his head.

'He hear something?' queried Cole.

They both listened. It took a few seconds for Cassidy to detect it, but she finally caught the sound of a cellphone ringing. She knew it wasn't the one she usually used, because it rested on the kitchen table. There was only one other in the cabin.

She bounced up from the couch, dashed into her bedroom, and straight for the chest of drawers at the rear of the room. She pulled open the top one, pushed aside a collection of shirts, and saw the burner phone that Jimmy had given her five years ago lit up and emitting an annoying jingle. She snatched it up, stared at it for a few more seconds, and then answered.

'Hello?' she whispered.

7

Butch Grissom slowly walked the semi-lit street. As he
paced from one end to the other and back again, he
continuously passed under a street light that seemed to
shut off for a few moments when he approached it, only
to snap back on after he had cleared it. He had observed
the phenomenon a few times in his life and had no
answer as to why it occurred and little interest in seeking
one. Maybe he was electrically charged somehow, which
given the pent up nervous energy he felt inside would
not have come as a surprise. Or perhaps he was cursed,
an unseen malevolent spirit perched upon the light
playing games with him.

Grissom certainly felt cursed. A few hours previously,
he had borne witness to one of the biggest shit-shows
of his career. No, stop. He checked himself. Career was
the wrong word. Career was what he had had serving as
a Navy Seal for ten years and a marine for ten before
that. Ordinary people had careers and jobs, families and

homes, hobbies and lives. Grissom had none of that now. He was an ex-person, just a small cog in a vast machine. He had little knowledge of the full scale of its workings because that was the deliberate intent. Only The Triumvirate truly knew what mechanics whirred behind the curtains, or so they claimed. All that was required of Grissom was that he do his part, the part he had been recruited for, the part that would capitalize on almost twenty years of ferocious training and the blackest of black operations, the part that would serve the cause he had pledged his loyalty to. That was all that mattered, and whatever The Triumvirate said would aid the cause was what Grissom did, unquestioningly.

That was why he had spent the best part of two years working with Axel Archer as a member of his crew, grudgingly deferring to him even though Grissom had certainly acquired more military experience. But Archer was the expert, Archer was the boss, Archer was the man. And that was why The Triumvirate would be monumentally pissed that Archer was dead. It had been the unsought result of the events of a few hours back, unavoidable once Archer had drawn his weapon. It was the reason why Grissom had chain-smoked the past half-hour away as he walked from one end of the street to the other, rehearsing in his head how he would break the news.

Grissom stopped, stamped out the butt of an expired cigarette, and lit up another. He had to inform The Triumvirate and soon. The NYPD would have found Archer within moments of Grissom and his team exfiltrating from the scene on the jetty. Within hours they would have identified the body. Then an unholy mess would descend as to why a notorious convicted thief, sentenced to multiple life terms and supposedly locked away securely in prison, had, in fact, bled out next to the East River, free as a bird. Grissom cursed himself that they had been unable to retrieve Archer's body, but the time taken to do so would have risked their own capture, which would have been unacceptable. It was well beyond his pay grade how that circle would be squared, but the more time the powers-that-be had to formulate a plan, the better. Grissom threw away the barely-expired cigarette and headed towards a nondescript black van parked directly beneath the cursed street light. True to form, it flickered off as he approached, but he paid it no mind as he slid open the side door, hopped inside the van and slammed it shut behind him.

The interior was bathed in the eerie glow generated by numerous flatscreen monitors on screensaver mode and the small multicolored emissions from a variety of circuit panels and electronic equipment. It was the surveillance van the crew had used in previous scores and what had helped them locate Archer so quickly, assisted by the tracking device they had implanted in him. Grissom's two other crewmates, Foster and Marks, slid their small chairs away towards the van's front, knowing to give Grissom the space he needed without him having to ask. He could sense they were as anxious as he was, but like Grissom, they didn't show it on the surface.

Foster was a former US Army Ranger and remained rigid in his bearing and character, the top of his crew-cut hair flat enough to balance a plate upon and his frame sizable enough to help lead any NFL offensive line. As far as Grissom could tell, Foster's only interests outside their missions lay in working out, firing-off his vast personal collection of weaponry, and reading books and magazines that revolved around working out and firing weapons. He may have acted like a robot, but that ensured his loyalty and dedication were programmed in, or at least it seemed that way.

As for Marks, he was the only member of the team without a military past, a former LAPD robbery-homicide detective who had seemingly viewed his time in the police as training to make him a better criminal. A stylish corn-row haircut, goatee, and diamond earring merely hinted at Marks's preference for fine living in a world of tailored suits, fast cars, and faster women when he wasn't an active member of the crew. Of all of them, Archer aside, Grissom felt Marks to be the most motivated by money than any higher purpose. But he was sharp, knowledgeable, and professional when it counted. The periods when the crew were stood down, which could sometimes stretch into months, were for Marks to do with as he pleased as long as it didn't interfere with operations.

Grissom took a seat at the table of monitors and pushed aside a keyboard to make space for a laptop he pulled out of a small alcove underneath. He opened it and used the encrypted signal to transmit to The Triumvirate that he was ready to talk when they were. You didn't call the trio, they always called you, when they were good and ready and never before. Grissom, Foster, and Marks sat in silence for several nervous minutes until the laptop's encrypted video conferencing program started beeping. Would he accept the call? Damn right he would.

THE NAME OF THE GAME

The screen opened to reveal three separate portrait-style windows, indicating calls from different locations. Each displayed a completely blacked-out silhouette of a person, gently backlit. The gender of each was impossible to discern, so deliberately opaque were they. When Grissom had spoken to them on previous occasions, their voices were digitally distorted to likewise conceal basic characteristics. The only identifiers that distinguished the figures from each other were single Greek letters at the base of their video windows - A for Alpha, Γ for Gamma, and Ω for Omega. Alpha occupied the center frame, which Grissom had always assumed denoted leadership, as did ownership of the first letter of the Greek alphabet. Their authority was total, but without knowing their genders, Grissom had referred to them by their letters from the beginning, and they had not objected.

'Report,' ordered Alpha in a distorted voice familiar to any B-movie serial killer.

'I can't sugarcoat it,' sighed Grissom, readying himself for the reveal. 'Archer is dead. We tracked him down as fast as we could, but his mobility and training complicated matters. We finally got him at Dumbo, but he drew a weapon, fired, and we had no choice but to respond. We evacuated just before the authorities arrived. Regrettably, we were forced to leave him or risk capture, which would have compromised our entire operation.'

There was a brief moment of silence during which Grissom could hear his heart pounding in his ears, but he kept calm, his stare fixed on the screen.

'That is unfortunate. Very unfortunate,' said Alpha eventually. 'Is his death confirmed?'

'Even if he had armor underneath his jacket, I put a round through his carotid artery. There's no walking away from that.'

'Did you retrieve the package?'

'He didn't have it on his person,' replied Grissom. 'We checked him as thoroughly as we could in the time we had.'

'Do we have any idea what he may have done with it?' probed Gamma. 'He only escaped for a few hours. Surely the places where he could have hidden it are limited.'

'We're retracing the GPS record of the tracking device to try and ascertain that,' answered Grissom. 'However, the device had to be small enough to be practically inserted into him. Its power and transmitter could never give pinpoint accurate coordinates, more like a general idea with a radius of a few dozen meters. Now we'll try our best, but that son of a bitch hopped, skipped and jumped across half the goddamn city before we caught him. He could have given the package to anyone, hidden it in a damn beer bottle, or thrown it in the East River, though I doubt he'd have destroyed it.'

'What makes you so sure?' queried Omega.

'Because of his warning. Under no circumstances were we to harm any of his friends and family. Otherwise, he said he had enough dirt on us to release to the press and the Feds, to rain down biblical levels of shit on our heads.'

'Given the premium value our organization places on secrecy, that would present a problem, wouldn't you agree, Mr. Grissom?' asked Alpha rhetorically.

'Yes, I would,' he nodded.

'Is it possible he sent one of his daughters the package, to guarantee their safety against reprisal?' posited Omega.

'It's certainly possible,' acknowledged Grissom with a shrug. 'We won't know until at least tomorrow though, and that's only if he sent it to one of the younger two we have under surveillance. As for the older two, they're ghosts. Then there's Delgado, his old army buddy. I can round up whoever's available right now, though, start pulling fingernails.'

'I want you to stand down for the time being,' said Alpha.

'Excuse me?' checked Grissom.

'If Archer's intent was to ensure his loved ones' protection, he would keep them as far from our interests as possible. Likewise, even if he disposed of the package, I see no utility in your team scrabbling about the city emptying out trash cans and probing drains for an item so small. Even if it were out there, you could search for months and find nothing.'

'But the time and expense to acquire that information!' objected Gamma.

'You'll hear no disagreement from me,' conceded Alpha. 'Mr. Archer's conscience, or whatever motivated his betrayal, has proven to be by far the costliest aspect of our endeavors. However, the world is always how we find it, seldom how we wish it. We shall have to attempt to acquire the information again, or as close as we can get given how rare the opportunity was the first time. And even then, we shall need a new team leader.'

Grissom grunted sharply, almost as if the dent to his pride had manifested itself physically.

'Alpha, respectfully, I'm perfectly capable-'

'Of fulfilling what is required of you,' interjected Alpha. 'And we require you and the team to defer to someone with the unique skills, experience, and dare I say imagination to plan, oversee, and execute the tasks we have in mind. We had access to such a person over the last two years. Now he lies dead on a slab and has become a problem demanding of our immediate attention. Return to your shadows, await instruction.'

With that, the call disconnected, and the screen returned to its desktop mode.

'Well shit, that was us told,' observed Marks with a sigh of relief.

'What do we do now?' asked Foster as he switched his gaze between the other two men, hoping for guidance.

Grissom reached for the pack of cigarettes inside his jacket pocket and noticed his hand was trembling slightly. He stretched his fingers out several times, and it stopped.

'You heard them. Stand down and wait out, same as between all the other jobs. Only this time, check your back more often, just in case someone's fixing to put a bullet in it.'

8

Within a second of the punch connecting, Delilah tasted blood. She stumbled backward, dazed, but managed to shake it off in time to duck and avoid her opponent's follow-on swing. The heavyweight female biker certainly had mass and power on her side, a collection of demonic tattoos and an ugly snarl adding to the intimidating persona. Not that Delilah had felt unsure about the fight in any way. As soon as she saw the walking concrete wall enter the caged arena, cheered on by dozens of hairy, bearded male onlookers, Delilah relished the challenge she was presented with.

Her ducking avoidance allowed her to sharply jab the biker lady in the ribs, which only seemed to enrage her further. Delilah was cocky but not stupid. She knew if her opponent got a proper hold on her, she would be pummeled into a pulp. Apart from no eye-gouging or crotch shots, the cage was a lawless land where anything was permitted short of killing your opponent. It was what made it so appealing for Delilah, to dance with danger once again, the pay-off being a high that could top any drug.

For such a huge lady, she was faster than Delilah had anticipated. She swung her fist wildly in a rage and caught Delilah's cheek. She felt her teeth rattle and saw a line of blood droplets spatter across the arena floor. She wobbled slightly, closed her eyes to regain her composure, and suddenly started laughing. Delilah had no idea where it came from, but suddenly she was in hysterics. Perhaps the last punch had finally knocked free her remaining loose screw. Still, she genuinely felt elated as she reveled in the pain, degradation, and self-destruction.

Even with her eyes closed, Delilah could sense the biker lady stomping towards her, ready to make the kill. She opened her eyes, leaped at the biker, grabbed both of the latter's firm shoulders, and pulled herself forwards. Delilah slammed her forehead into the biker's face, crushing her nose in a small eruption of blood and cartilage. The biker howled in agony and toppled backward like a fallen tree trunk. Delilah rode her downwards and found herself straddling the woman as she lay prostrate on the ground. Delilah was free to repeatedly slam her fists into an increasingly pulverized biker head. She made the most of the opportunity. Even as blood spattered across her face, she never stopped laughing. However, if the bloodthirsty crowd had quietened rather than cheered, they would have heard several sobs intrude.

Outside, amidst the lines of motorcycles, was parked Delilah's Gran Torino. In the trunk, the interior of a half-opened bag lit up as a cellphone started ringing. It went unanswered.

**

Bethany put down the cellphone she had rarely picked up in five years and struggled not to vomit. She leaned over the kitchen sink of the penthouse apartment and breathed deeply. She reached for a glass, filled it with water, and drank greedily, gasping as she finished. Bethany wiped her mouth with her fluffy bathrobe's sleeve and stared out the window across the Manhattan skyline. Her thoughts raced, jumping from numbness to disbelief, to despair, to rage and back to numbness. In truth, it had felt like her father had already been lost to her for five years, a fading memory, just a ghost who never had a funeral. But Bethany had known that he was still out there somewhere, languishing in prison but nevertheless alive. So it had been an abstract feeling, able to be shelved as she attempted to navigate the uncharted waters of her new life.

Now Axel was dead, and it wasn't so abstract anymore. Jimmy's voice, already stunning to Bethany's ears after so long unheard, had delivered the news as delicately as he could have under the circumstances. Naturally, she had insisted on knowing more, but Jimmy repeated the same thing he said he had told Cassidy in conversation and Delilah via voicemail. Axel was gone, killed by forces unknown, and that he would call back soon with a place and time to meet. It was the only sensible way to proceed. Until then, hang tight and stay safe.

Hang tight, he had said. Maybe it would be easier than Bethany thought. Emotionally processing not just Axel's death, but the consequent resurrection of Bethany Archer from the void would dominate her thoughts in the short term, certainly enough to temporarily keep anxiety and impatience at bay.

'Mommy, I'm done,' came Lily's voice from behind Bethany.

She turned to the kitchen table to see that the little girl had finished her small breakfast bowl of yogurt and berries, a half-finished glass of milk to the side. While she had David's sharp blue eyes, she took after Bethany in most other ways, her hair the same chestnut brown.

'That's good, sweetheart,' said Bethany as she sniffed back the tears that she simply couldn't contain. 'Finish your milk, and you can go play a little before nursery, okay?'

David walked into the kitchen, attempting to knot the tie of his business suit as he went, preparing for a rare Saturday meeting.

'Morning munchkin,' he greeted Lily with a kiss on her forehead.

He headed towards Bethany, who approached him and started on his tie herself.

'How's my other princess this morning?' he queried cheerfully. However, he quickly shifted to a concerned tone when he saw Bethany's lips quiver. 'What's wrong?'

'Nothing, I'm okay,' she responded unconvincingly.

'Nuh-uh,' countered David as he shook his head. 'We don't do this, remember? No games.'

Bethany gave up on his tie and burst into tears. She quickly left the room to avoid upsetting Lily. As she stood next to a window in the adjacent lounge, she heard David reassuring a curious Lily that mommy had something in her eye. He needed to help her out for a minute, but Lily could go play in her room until he took her to nursery. He entered the lounge and placed a hand on Bethany's shoulder. She turned around and buried her face into his chest, bawling as he wrapped his arms around her reassuringly.

'It's okay, I'm here,' he whispered. 'Tell me, what's wrong?'

Anger swelled inside Bethany that she could not even hint at the truth to the man she loved. The risk was too great that the whole tapestry she had weaved over the last five years would begin to unravel. She had everything she had ever wanted and yet felt completely helpless and alone. The unfairness of it all galled her. However, she had made a choice, and just as every choice had consequences, this one had caught up with her, leaving no option but to lie yet again. She gently pulled away and shook her head.

'I'm just overreacting, that's all. I didn't have a good day with the ladies yesterday.'

'You didn't say anything last night?' queried David.

'I didn't want to bother you with it. Most of them are fine, it's just a few of them, but I'll deal with it. I'm not some kid on the school yard.'

'Just give it time, their behavior will catch up with them in the end,' said David reassuringly. 'Karma's a bitch.'

Don't I know it, thought Bethany. Despite her best hopes, she also somehow knew that karma wasn't done with her yet.

***

Angie finished tying her running shoes and started jogging on the spot. She had slept badly, still upset about her encounter with Jimmy the previous evening. A run in the Saturday morning air would help clear her head. Most students had returned home for the weekend or weren't even out of bed yet, so she was assured some peace and quiet. She would then eat a late breakfast and catch a train into the city to pass on last night's digital haul to her occasional partner, Ziggy, an eccentric but harmless hacker and information dealer. She would get what was owed to her, Jimmy be damned.

She stopped as she rounded the corner of the main building and saw Jimmy standing next to his SUV. Immediately she knew something was different. He was dressed normally, not in a suit, nor was there any sign of an expensive car. He had dispensed with his cover. More to the point, he looked sad. Not just down, but truly saddened, as close to tears as stoic males got without giving in to them. She slowed her jog to a walk and approached him.

'What's wrong, tell me,' she demanded.

Jimmy knew not to mess her around.

'I'm sorry, hon, but he's gone.'

Angie instantly knew what he meant, but the first place her mind went was not to images of her father, but to her parting words to Jimmy the previous evening, which took on new and acutely painful relevance.

I'd have been better off as an orphan.

She closed her eyes, but no matter how hard she wished it to be so, it was no dream, and there was no waking up from it.

9

For all the brutality, savagery, carnage and inhumanity Jorge Melendez had witnessed in over five decades on earth, whether in his youth and military career in his native Colombia or more latterly as an 'advisor' to *Los Escorpiones* cartel in Mexico, even he had to wince at the sight playing out before him. Melendez, half a dozen members of the inner circle, and the cartel's leader, Pablo Guzman, stood before a huge internet-connected smart TV as it showed a newly posted video on social media. The video's subject was Guzman's younger brother, Ernesto, tied to a chair, sweating, gagged, and naked. He was almost hyperventilating in terror as his masked tormentor revved up a chainsaw and, with barely a pause for thought, tore into him. As the sound of Ernesto's muffled screams mixed in with and then gave way to the sickening sound of metal pulverizing flesh and bone, Melendez turned away. It was not because the sight disturbed him - he had become desensitized years ago - but because it was superfluous to simply stand and watch when he knew that work needed to be done. He produced his phone from his thousand-dollar suit and tapped out a message to his men to ready themselves for imminent orders.

Melendez pocketed the phone and stared at himself in the nearby gold-trimmed mirror, which complemented the expensive but gaudy furniture and decor of the rest of the room, enough to make even a Middle Eastern dictator blush. Even though he needed to dye his lush, swept-back hair and neatly-trimmed beard to disguise the grey that had been encroaching since his mid-thirties, Melendez was still pleasantly surprised his body had held up so well. His olive skin was far less blemished than men of similar age, and his midriff only carried a slight paunch rather than a full-on gut. Abandoning his role as a colonel in Colombian military intelligence to work freelance for the Mexicans a decade earlier had, at the time, significantly reduced his stress and increased his bank balance. The former had helped his mindfulness, and the latter had allowed some cosmetic surgeries. Together they combined to help keep the ravages of age at bay.

That said, despite the comfortable early period, Melendez's mental and physical wellbeing were being put under increased pressure by his employer's recent behavior. The money was phenomenal, but so was the stress of continually having to clean up messes and save Guzman from his own actions, to get him to think strategically and rationally in his battles with the rival cartels. The man was ruthless and intelligent, two qualities essential to reaching the top of any organization, but he was also a psychopath, capable of ice-cold casual cruelty and volcanically explosive acts of violence. As Guzman had become more paranoid and unhinged, the violence had more often than not taken a front seat. He would retreat to the dungeons beneath his expansive villa in Mexico's Sonora Province and indulge in filming sadistic torture scenes involving captured enemies. Melendez could not help but grin inside at the

THE NAME OF THE GAME

poetic justice of the much-beloved Ernesto succumbing to the same fate that Pablo had inflicted upon dozens of others. Any amusement was short-lived, though. Melendez wondered, as he was increasingly minded to do, how soon it would be until Guzman's paranoia made a snuff-film star of the Colombian himself. Doubtless would come the day when Melendez would either have to vanish or put down Guzman like the rabid dog he was. But that day was not yet here.

Melendez turned around when he heard an almighty crash. He saw that Guzman, a wiry, long-haired fox of a man, had ripped the television from the wall and thrown it to the marble floor. The Colombian looked on dispassionately as his boss flew into a screaming tantrum, grabbing anything fragile and not nailed down. He threw them at the floor, at walls, occasionally at some of the inner circle, who cautiously backed away as best they could without looking like they wanted to run. Melendez knew it was best to leave Guzman to exhaust himself like an overactive five-year-old, and after a few moments, he indeed collapsed to the floor, sweating and crying in despair. Whatever else could be said of Guzman, he had virtually raised his younger brother and loved him dearly. The resulting wrath would fall upon the perpetrators with the force of a tsunami.

'How did this happen?' demanded a panting Guzman.

'He was snatched at his favorite strip joint,' replied Melendez. 'He was led away by some piece of ass and ordered his bodyguards to give him some privacy. Soon after, my two men were beaten unconscious, and when they awoke, Ernesto was gone. Don't blame them, Pablo. They are competent and loyal and do as they are told. Unlike your brother. I warned Ernesto it was not wise to party in Vegas. Too many opportunities to get to him. But he would not listen.'

Melendez was aware that he was treading the finest of lines. Still, one of the reasons Guzman had hired him, had praised Melendez during his saner moments, was that, unlike the rest of the inner circle, the Colombian was not a yes man and refused to be one. That respect for speaking truth to power had frayed lately as Guzman had grown drunk on it. Still, just enough regard for honesty resided amidst the narco's paranoia that Melendez felt he could make his point, if nothing else to stop Guzman ordering that his men be killed. Yes, there was fraternal loyalty to them, many of whom Melendez had personally recruited from South and Central American militaries and intelligence agencies. However, on a purely practical level, such recruitment efforts would not be helped in the future if word got out that their prospective boss was liable to feed recruits to dogs if they incurred his displeasure.

'Are you saying this was my brother's fault?' hissed Guzman, his eyes widening.

You're damn right I am, the cocky little shit, thought Mclendez.

'I'm saying my advice is worth nothing if it's not listened to,' he responded coolly.

Guzman stared at him a moment, fire in his eyes. He eventually licked his teeth and picked himself up.

'I will deal with *Los Chacales*. They took Ernesto, the fuckers. They didn't even try to hide it, boasting of it online, rubbing my face in his blood.'

'I'll start assembling my team,' said Melendez as he reached for his phone.

'Uh uh,' said Guzman as he shook his head and wagged a finger. 'I will take your men, no, *all* of our men, and personally wipe those dogs from the face of the earth.'

Melendez tried to conceal his surprise. For months *Los Escorpiones* and *Los Chacales* had been engaging in a war of attrition against each other in bloody competition for the lucrative drug trafficking routes into the South Western United States. Thanks to careful intelligence gathering, planning, and targeted operations as directed by Melendez, *Los Escorpiones* were gradually gaining the upper hand, and he had no doubt that they would eventually triumph. Now Pablo seemed to want to take all his chips and bet them on blood red.

'This is most unwise, Pablo,' responded Melendez as calmly as he could. 'We've been relatively discrete so far, minimum civilian casualties, which has worked well enough for us. But start leaving trails of bullets and bodies in the crossfire of this little crusade and the Federal Police, even the military, will be down on us before we know it. There are only so many we can bribe.'

It was pointless. He could instantly tell that any argument would be futile. Pablo's blood was up, and only bloodletting would satisfy that lust.

'I hear you, Jorge, but I need to do this. As for you, I have the most important task.'

'More important than launching an all-out war against our biggest rival?'

'Oh, yes. I want you to find out who kidnapped my brother.'

'Well, it was *Los Chacales*, clearly,' responded Melendez, slightly confused.

Guzman stepped over and stood unnervingly close to Melendez, their faces only inches apart. He gently brushed his fingers across the Colombian's shoulder, dusting away some imaginary lint.

'No, no, no,' clucked Guzman. 'I mean find out *exactly* who it was. Their names, their faces, everything.'

'Respectfully Pablo, that's a tall order. They will be well away with the wind by now.'

'Just do it!' screamed Guzman. 'You're supposed to have been an intelligence officer, so I expect a little fucking intelligence for my money, understand!'

'Clear as a bell,' replied Melendez, his ears ringing slightly from Guzman's audio assault so close to his face.

He used his thumb to discreetly wipe some spittle from his cheek. However, if it had been a different time, a different place, Melendez would have happily jammed the thumb into Guzman's eye socket and forced it into his brain for such an act of disrespect.

'And if I find out who they are, then what?' he queried.

Guzman stepped away and started pacing around in a small circle, his hands formed into a pyramid under his nose. When he spoke, he did so calmly and quietly.

'No matter how long it takes, whether it be weeks, months, or years, you chase them to the ends of the earth, you kick over every rock they hide under until they have nowhere left to run. You destroy their lives, kill everyone they love, or have ever loved. Make their existence a scorched earth of despair. Finally, when they are truly broken, bring them to me. I am Pablo Rodriguez Guzman, and I will have my revenge, personally.'

Melendez gazed at Guzman a moment, marveling at how the man seemingly jumped in and out of sanity like a mental game of hopscotch. He pulled out his phone to arrange a flight to Las Vegas.

'Consider it done, Pablo. Consider it done.'

To be continued in...

VOLUME ONE, PART TWO
SISTERHOOD

Tragedy sees the Archer sisters return to New York City, reunited for the first time in five years, emotions still raw even after so long spent apart. However, differences are put aside when Axel Archer's final message to his daughters contains a warning not to investigate his death but to carry on with their lives.

It is a warning that the sisters cannot follow, for love, loyalty, and honor demand that they discover who took their father's life and make them pay. Whoever recruited Axel needed the skills of one of the best thieves available. So the sisters resolve to become as good if not better a recruitment prospect to find out how deep the rabbit hole goes. Their path to revenge will not be traveled as the Archers, though, but as the newest, slickest, and most effective heist crew in New York City - The Brooklyn Queens.

But first, they will need to save Jimmy Delgado from a vengeful mobster, while avoiding the attentions of NYPD detective Bryan Becker, who has his own reasons for investigating Axel's murder. Meanwhile, drug cartel enforcer Jorge Melendez arrives in Las Vegas to begin his hunt for the woman who kidnapped his employer's murdered brother, and no one who had any dealings with her will have forgotten Delilah Archer...

In the same shared universe...

Dark River

An Amanda Northstar Mystery

Independence, a small town and county on the banks of
the Hudson River, is a typical, all-American community
with a proud history dating back to Colonial times. But
just like anywhere else it cannot escape the darker side
of human nature. Murder, violence, corruption; these
and other crimes are not the exception in Independence.
But Sheriff Amanda Northstar is determined that they
don't become the rule.

When the body of Judy Sterling, one of Independence's
most prominent councilors, washes up on the bank of
the Hudson the first assumption is suicide. With her car
abandoned near the county's main bridge, a suicide note

left inside, it seems that Judy willingly jumped to her death.

However, Amanda's intuition tells her that there is far more to Judy's death than first appears. As more evidence emerges and Amanda and her deputies piece together the growing collection of clues, they discover that Judy was caught up in a web of lies, desperation, betrayal and perhaps even murder.

Ḟeads Will Roll

An Amanda Northstar Mystery

As Independence prepares for Halloween weekend, houses and streets are decorated with carved pumpkins, fake tombstones, and fun monsters. The town also plays host to a festival celebrating the best of horror literature. Authors, poets, and academics from around the country mix with fans, with an open-air theatrical production of *The Legend of Sleepy Hollow* launching the event.

Sheriff Amanda Northstar and her deputies, Jake Murrow and Casey Norris, police proceedings as audience anticipation builds for the appearance of the Headless Horseman. When the Horseman finally rides in, everyone enjoys the show until the pumpkin-headed actor falls to the ground, and it is discovered that he has been genuinely decapitated inside his mask.

As the weekend unfolds, more bodies are discovered around Independence, each murder influenced by a famous horror tale. With the clock ticking down to Halloween night, Amanda, Jake, and Casey race to discover what links the victims and stop an insanely imaginative killer from realizing a truly devilish design.

ABOUT THE AUTHOR

IJ Benneyworth is a British writer with a long academic and personal appreciation for American history and culture, strengthened by repeated visits to the U.S. He has been writing creatively in one form or another since he was a child, first practicing his story-craft by improvising adventure tales around the fireplace with his grandfather, to having his stories read out in class during his school years.

He moved into screenwriting and filmmaking after graduating from university, and worked in various production office and crew roles in the film and television industry for several years. In recent years IJ has moved back to writing short stories and novels, as well as becoming an academic in the field of International Relations and Security Studies.

Dark River was his first published novel, and the first to feature Amanda Northstar, the sheriff of Independence, a fictional town and county on the banks of the Hudson River, inspired by his wonderful visits to many of the towns and villages of the region, as well as the Catskill Mountains. The second book in the Amanda Northstar mysteries series, *Heads Will Roll*, soon followed, and he is currently working on the third in the series, *Blindsided*.

Over time IJ will be expanding the fictional universe Amanda inhabits with novels following other characters who occupy the same world but operate in different parts of the United States, following their own adventures and story arcs, such as the *Queens of the Steal* series of novellas.